AGATHA ANXIOUS

& THE

DEER ISLAND GHOST

Wyatt & Sons Publishers books may be ordered through booksellers or by contacting:

Wyatt & Sons Publishers, LLC
Mobile, Alabama 36695
www.wyattpublishing.com
editor@wyattpublishing.com

Because of the dynamic nature of the Internet, any web address or links contained in this book may have changed since publication and may no longer be valid.

ISBN 13:978-1-954798-34-2
Printed in the United States of America

AGATHA ANXIOUS

& THE

DEER ISLAND GHOST

RJ McDOWELL

Book 1 of **The Deadfellow Five**

WYATT & SONS
PUBLISHERS, LLC
Mobile, Alabama

PRAISE FOR RJ MCDOWELL
&
AGATHA ANXIOUS

"If you like spooky MG you should pick this book up. Think Goosebumps meets City of Ghosts."

Jessica Kahle, Goodreads

"This is the perfect book for younger readers who enjoy scary stories. This is a great start to what promises to be a great series! I think it would be a great addition to any classroom and school library."

Rachel, Goodreads

"Full of twists and turns, spooks and screams this is a fun "lled story that I couldn't put down and you wouldn't want to miss out on."

Kirsty Carson, NetGalley

"A spine-tingling tale with a good-natured plot, a determined heroine, and a few twists that will surely give you a chill. Middle school grade thriller/horror reminiscent of my years reading R.L Stine."

A. Tompkins, NetGalley

"This is an absolute must-read for any young adult, or even adult."

Katherine Burgess, Goodreads

"Whispers of darkness, darkened cemeteries and creepy haunts, with even darker mysteries that defy sight and beckon the curious to see into the nightshade. Agatha Anxious took me down a delightful eerie pilgrimage through twisting unknowns, anxious imagination, and ful!ll-ment of her discovery quest."

David J. Chavers, Goodreads

"Welcome to Biloxi, Mississippi, where southern charm and spooky ghosts abound! R.J. McDowell does an excep□tional job bringing this sleepy coastal town to life."

Sarah, Goodreads

"R.J. McDowell creates a #awlessly eerie world in which her characters interact. She builds suspense effortlessly, with the end of each chapter insisting you read the next... and the next."

Jenn Anne Becker, NetGalley

For Aunt Cindy.
Death is no thief of your magic.

And for Mr. Maters.
Your carbon-based human life form Kept It Simple Stupid.

"Don't wait until the sun doth set
to visit the shop of Blanche Caillavet.
A riddle she'll ask to sell you a mask.
You and your soul are the debt."

— UNKNOWN

PROLOGUE

The truth may hurt for a little while,
but a lie hurts forever.

Summer, 1964

It was late in the afternoon, right before closing, when two Biloxi policemen appeared at the door of one of the city's oldest and most beloved establishments: Blanche's Baubles & Beads. The heat, coupled with equal parts reluctance and hesitation, produced beads of sweat on the officers' necks.

The older one slapped a mosquito away. "Let's get on with it."

The bell over the door signaled their entrance, and they were greeted with one of the town's prettiest yet aged faces. She didn't smile.

"Blanche Caillavet," the younger one said, putting his hands on his belt in a show of dominance.

"Yes?" the old woman said immediately, unintimidated.

"We have a search warrant for your business."

She gritted her teeth. "I didn't do a thing to that boy you're looking for."

"This was the last place he was known to be," the older officer interrupted. "And that's all that matters." He laid the paper on the counter in front of her.

She pushed it away. "I have a lot of children who come in here. I don't remember him."

11

The officers ignored her and set about their work, searching corners and cabinets of the small Mardi Gras shop, looking through the shelves, peering behind the curtains, checking the bathroom, poking their noses in every nook and cranny, searching for something—anything—that belonged to Bobby Calvert.

"What are these, ma'am?" The younger officer pointed to a row of boxes lining a shelf in the back workroom where multiple unfinished masks, paints, ribbons, and brushes littered a wooden worktable.

Blanche Caillavet considered not answering him but thought better of it. "I keep my supplies in there. You're welcome to look, Officer—" She read his name off his uniform. "Webb. You were going to anyway, weren't you?"

Officer Webb pointed his finger at her. "Go sit down behind your register, Ms. Caillavet, and let us do our work here. Ladner!" he bossed the older officer. "Keep eyes on her."

Officer Ladner lumbered to the cash register desk, where Blanche was now seated. He tried to be gentle. "I'm really sorry about this, ma'am. I hope you understand."

"Of course, I don't," Blanche said emphatically, her arms crisscrossed over her petite frame, her blondish-grey hair in a severe bun at the nape of her neck. "My family's been in this town for far too long to be accused of something like this."

"Nobody is accusing you, ma'am," Officer Ladner said. "Let us do our duty. The boy's friends say he stopped by your shop that night. I mean, how do we know you didn't do something to him and have your father cremate him at his funeral home?" Suddenly he'd stopped being delicate.

Blanche narrowed her eyes. "Why would I do something to the boy? I'm telling you, he was never in this shop!"

"Then what is this?"

Officer Ladner and Blanche Caillavet turned to face Officer Webb, who now held a small watch in his gloved hand.

"What is that?" Blanche squinted to see the item in his hand.

Officer Webb didn't answer her. Instead, he set it on the counter in front of her. The backside had a small engraving, cursive letters clearly displaying the word "Bobby."

Officer Webb pulled out a pair of handcuffs. "I'll tell you what it is. It's called PROOF, Ms. Caillavet."

CHAPTER 1
AN UNSETTLING SECRET

The sky darkened as Agatha Anxious neared her favorite place, the Old Biloxi Cemetery. The wind weaved itself among the moss-lined oaks, rustling the last of the remaining October leaves. With no one around to impress, she breathed a sigh of relief. Being alone had its perks.

The cemetery was on her way home from school—not to mention her backyard faced the cemetery, and she could see the graves from her bedroom window—so she came, five days a week, to run her fingers along the tops of headstones. She read names and dates engraved in the stone and sat motionless for hours on the dirt pondering the bones buried beneath her.

She liked the hundreds of graves, especially the older ones dating back several centuries. The crumbling, barely legible structures represented a tale—a history. Every body in the graveyard had a story, she knew. Her uncle was buried here, and his grave was always her last visit before heading home. She'd been told he'd died in the war, having accidentally stepped on some sort of mine, which exploded. Agatha could figure out the rest. Her father, Sonny, once told her parts of him were

14

fake at his funeral. Picturing her uncle lying in his casket, dressed in his uniform with parts of him missing, had kept Agatha up for days.

Still, something kept her coming to his grave every day after school. Like he was beckoning her.

Agatha knew she was different, a truth she secretly liked. Her family had very little money, and her mother made all her clothes. Once a month, Mama took Agatha to the local fabric store to choose two patterns and fabric. The patterns were always a dress, and her materials of choice were black, dark grey, or navy. No buttons, ribbons, or bows. Agatha coupled each dress with a pair of black stockings she usually tore within the first couple weeks of wearing them. However, Mrs. Anxious wouldn't replace them until the next month's fabric store visit.

Agatha's bobbed blonde hair, cut by her mother's zig-zag fabric scissors, was always uneven. One side of her hair lay longer than the other, with her bangs at a depressing, downhill slope. The Mississippi humidity put a kink in it that no straightener, flat iron, or amount of prayer could undo. Her family had no money for either flat irons or straighteners anyway. And Agatha didn't care about having name-brand clothes. Still, she did wonder if some of the whispers at school were because of her unusual fashion choices.

Maybe it wasn't her appearance that garnered the stares and whispers. Perhaps it was her nervous nature. Agatha had the unlovely habit of biting her nails to the quick, always worried about something. And when her fingers weren't in her mouth, one hand usually picked at the other, ripping away some skin or snagging a cuticle. She hid her habit under the dinner table, behind her back, or under her desk at school until, fingers bleeding, she wiped them on her dress. Dark fabric was excellent at hiding bloodstains.

What she did care about were pockets. More than anything, Agatha wanted a dress with pockets. Pockets would be much easier to hide her ragged, bloody fingers. When Agatha requested pockets be added, her mother shrugged her off, giving her a hundred reasons why that wouldn't happen. Mama hadn't learned how to make pockets when she'd learned to sew. Mama was a very busy lady who didn't have time to learn anything new. Mama didn't want to purchase additional material. Agatha still had hope. Her thirteenth birthday was tomorrow, and she planned to ask again.

A soft drizzle trickled from a few angry clouds as Agatha left Irish Hill Drive, turning onto Caldwell Avenue toward her uncle's grave. An autumn breeze tickled her legs, winding itself like a snake down the neck of her navy dress, passing her belly button, and circling its forked tongue around the knee holes in her stockings. She shuddered, wrapping her arms around herself. The rain stung her eyes, so she looked down at her blackened shoes as she walked. White shoes were the only ones her mother could afford, so Agatha covered them with silver duct tape and colored the tape with a black marker to give them character. The wet ground caused some of the tape to loosen, and Agatha bent down, pressing it hard against the shoe, but the tape wouldn't obey.

"Hi."

Agatha heard a voice in front of her, and she fell backward into the grass, soaking the bottom of her dress. She wasn't alone.

"I'm sorry. I didn't mean to scare you," a nervous-looking boy said. He was leaning against her uncle's headstone and playing with his earlobe, rubbing it between his thumb and forefinger.

Agatha huffed, wiping herself off. Dark fabric was good at hiding dirt too. She recognized him as the loner boy, Leopold Panic, from her seventh-grade History and English classes. He was the boy no one talked to, and he mostly kept to himself. He looked uncomfortably at her, his green eyes darting left and right and up and down like balls in a pinball machine. He wore a stiff, collared shirt neatly tucked into a pair of jeans and had completed his look with a matching yellow bow tie. Agatha wondered if his family was in some sort of religious cult that required them to dress that way. Amish, she thought, although she wasn't sure any Amish were in Mississippi. Wait, didn't the Amish wear black? Leopold wasn't wearing black. Whatever it was, she didn't care. She did care, however, where Leopold happened to be standing.

"That is my uncle's grave," she said cooly.

"Oh. Sorry," he said, moving his tall, slender body away from the stone. He brushed off the area he'd been touching and sat on the edge of a nearby stone bench, politely leaving enough room for Agatha. "I didn't realize."

Leopold tucked a wisp of his brown hair behind his ear and pulled a couple of times on his other earlobe. "I, uh, took a shortcut through here." He smiled awkwardly, exposing one front tooth that stuck out ever so slightly in front of the other. Agatha had never seen him smile. In school, he usually sat hunched over his desk, doodling something in a notebook, altogether ignoring the teacher or that day's lesson. Agatha knew very little about Leopold, but she knew enough to think he was strange.

Agatha liked strange.

"I come here every day," she said, planting herself on the bench next to him—but not too close—one leg swinging nervously underneath her. A weird silence passed between them.

"I like cemeteries," he said, looking off in the distance toward the older graves near Biloxi beach. "People are scared of them, but I'm not."

"Same," Agatha said, trying to sound cool. A twinge of excitement rose in her belly. No one liked the cemetery the way she did. "I mean, the stories that are here, you know? I wonder a lot about how people died. Like, was it a gross death? Was anybody in here murdered? Or even better, was somebody in here a murder-er?" She emphasized the last syllable in a way that made her uneasy. "That's kind of evil, isn't it?"

"No, I get it. Sometimes I make up stories for them."

"Me too!" Agatha squealed, hopping off the bench. She leaned against a nearby mausoleum bearing the last name Ainsworth. "Especially the children. If I find a kid's grave, I imagine some crazy story about how they died. Like this one," she said, motioning to the stone structure behind her. "The whole family is in this one. One daughter died in 1914 at the age of eight. What do you think?"

Leopold rested his chin on his fist in an exaggerated way as if deep in thought. "Black Plague."

Agatha rolled her eyes. "Come on. The Black Plague was way before 1914."

"Oh. Diarrhea, then. Diarrhea's been around forever." Agatha's eyes widened before they both erupted in laughter.

Leopold's cheeks flushed red. "Maybe," Agatha said at last. She turned back toward the mausoleum. "Pneumonia. Something simple like that."

"Probably," Leopold agreed.

Agatha ran her fingers along the smooth marble as she thought hard about something. "Hey, do you think they ever come back?"

Leopold Panic snapped his head up, taking in a breath that was more of a gasp. His mouth hung open, and he tugged at his bowtie, scratching the skin under the stiff white collar until three pink lines formed. "What...what do you mean?" He tried to maintain his composure.

Agatha put her pinky in her mouth, tearing at the edge of the skin around the cuticle. "Um, I dunno. Like, you know, ghosts."

Before she knew it, the stone bench was empty. Leopold stormed past her with a purpose she didn't understand, his brown boots stomping in the squishy grass beside her. "I, uh, need to be home. It's almost four o'clock."

"What did I say?" Agatha called after him, irritated. "I thought you liked cemeteries. You scared?" The words left her lips before she could stop them, a regular occurrence for Agatha.

Leopold froze with his back to her. It was raining harder than before, the heavy droplets soaking his brown, perfectly combed hair. He turned and walked back to her, head down. "I live a couple of streets over from here. I've seen you walk among the graves after school. I've... been wanting to talk to you. I thought you might understand since I know you come here every day."

The rain clung to his long eyelashes.

"Understand what?" She looked up at him, suddenly uneasy. He was much taller than she'd realized. She took a small step backward.

Leopold bit his lip before continuing and tucked another wisp of hair behind his ear. "It's my grandfather. He sits on the end of my bed every night. He comes into my room when he thinks I'm asleep and just sits in the dark. I know he's there because I can hear him breathing. He doesn't move, but he does talk to me. A little. Mostly, he just squeezes my foot and says, 'You're a good boy, Leopold.'" Leopold looked down at his hands, picking something sticky off his left palm.

Agatha narrowed her eyes. "Okay? I mean, that's creepy, but what's wrong with that?"

Leopold put his hands in the pockets of his jeans, nervously rustling some loose change. Pockets, Agatha thought enviously, her mind wandering.

"You don't understand, Agatha," he replied. "My grandfather died five years ago."

CHAPTER 2
RED RUM ROW

Agatha managed a small half-smile, acknowledging Leopold's words as a joke, but she soon saw it was no prank. He didn't smile back, only sucked in a breath as if to stifle a cry. Unsure what to say or do, she broke into a sprint, flying from the cemetery as if her ankles had wings and her fluttering heart was their motor. She ran from where she'd come, toward the front exit where the older cemetery inhabitants had taken up residency centuries before. Her feet sunk into mud puddles, splashing the graves' dark brown dirt onto her stockings and shoes. She expertly wound her way through the crumbling headstones and mausoleums until she reached the exit, flinging herself toward the cemetery's iron gates until they swung open with a reluctant groan.

Once outside, she walked along Beach Boulevard in a daze, one lone thumb in her mouth. The gulf was particularly rough this afternoon, the tips of the water forming white caps before crashing onto the shore. A storm was coming. Perhaps it's already here, Agatha thought, a peach size pit of worry in her stomach. Cars raced past her left and right, their occupants in a hurry as if a hurricane were coming. Everyone in Biloxi was always in a hurry during a big storm.

She bit off a piece of her fingernail and played with it between her teeth. Why would Leopold tell me that? I don't even know him. A chill crept up her spine, like a skeleton's fingers counting each of her vertebrae, one by one, until it reached the base of her skull, where it spread open its bony hand across her scalp. She shivered as she walked two more blocks to the second stop of her daily after-school routine.

Hattie's Odds & Ends was another of Agatha's favorite places—second only to the cemetery. Pushing open the wooden door, Agatha found her favorite person, Aunt Hattie, sitting behind her sizeable antique desk, a fancy structure whose feet were carved in the shape of lions' paws. The end of a pen protruded from her mouth. Hattie was concentrating on something.

Agatha's father was Aunt Hattie's brother. There was only about a year and a half between them—something the Anxious family called "Irish Twins," a term Agatha didn't understand but knew it had something to do with them being so close in age. They were very close for a brother and sister. "As thick as thieves," Aunt Hattie would sometimes say, another phrase Agatha didn't quite grasp. What she did gather, though, was that even though they were very close, Aunt Hattie was a mysterious person. Agatha often felt she had quite a lot of secrets even her father didn't know about.

Aunt Hattie turned when she heard the door. "Well, hello, Miz Magnolia," she said to Agatha in an overdone southern drawl.

Agatha adored Aunt Hattie. She was a beautiful woman, in a witchy sort of way, Agatha thought. Thin and petite with long, straight grey hair that sometimes appeared blue in the right light. Tanned skin that had seen too many suns but managed to escape the wrinkles. Rosy lips, high cheekbones, and a dainty little nose encased a pair of dark brown eyes as warm and welcoming as a plate of cookies fresh from the oven. Thin arms and long bony fingers gave her a spidery appearance, but Agatha loved her creepy presence. Not to mention, Aunt Hattie was the only one in the family who never scolded her with a 'get your hands out of your mouth' or a slap on the hand when Agatha bit her nails. She hated the slap the most. Biting her nails was Agatha's business. Hers and hers alone.

Agatha decided to play along, despite her unease about Leopold. "Good afternoon, Miz Honeysuckle." She wasn't as good at the southern accent as Aunt Hattie. Even though Agatha was born and raised in Biloxi, she had escaped having a southern accent.

Aunt Hattie removed her blue-rimmed glasses from the end of her nose—a colorful, beaded chain dangled them from her neck— and looked Agatha up and down with a crooked smile. Aunt Hattie had pinned her grey hair in two tiny buns atop her head, giving her the appearance of horns. She pointed a slender finger at Agatha's feet. "I like the look."

Agatha glanced down, her stockings and shoes splattered with mud. "It started to rain. I ran all the way here."

Aunt Hattie gave a small laugh. "Looks like cemetery mud."

Agatha didn't bother to ask her how she knew. Aunt Hattie seemed to know a lot of things before Agatha had a chance to explain them. Like the day six years ago when her dog, Crutches, died. Agatha was still crying in her bedroom when Aunt Hattie stopped by to give her a few fresh-picked jonquils and a note that said, "I'm sorry. Heartworms suck." Or the time Agatha made her first B on a report card. Aunt Hattie invited her over that very evening for a large bowl of popcorn and two old black and white scary movies, their favorite thing to do together. Some things didn't need explanations. Aunt Hattie just knew.

Just then, the phone rang. "Let me get that." Aunt Hattie

clasped her hands together. "Have a look around. I have some new stuff."

Agatha nodded as Aunt Hattie answered the phone. "Hattie's Odds and Ends. What can I do for you?"

Her aunt's voice trailed off as Agatha started down one of the four aisles of items in Aunt Hattie's store. The store had been open for all of Agatha's life. It was made up of booths containing an odd collection of practically anything anybody could think of. Scary things, weird things, things one would never find anywhere else. Agatha started at the right side of the store and worked her way to the left. She always thought the odder and more disturbing things were at the left side of the store and wondered if Aunt Hattie had done that on purpose. A progression of creepiness and Agatha liked to save the best for last. Walking the aisles was like being in the pages of a ghost story. It only got weirder and darker as you went along.

Agatha tried to locate the new items. A taxidermy orange bat, its wings spread wide inside a small picture frame and its eyes still in their sockets, stared at her eye-level on a shelf. Its furry little body appeared soft to the touch; its mouth gaped open as if in a permanent scream. Beneath the bat, a pair of iron German Shepherd bookends stood at attention, sandwiching a trio of fat, colorful books so old the writing on the covers had worn away. An old record player, a cow skull, and a pair of salt and pepper shakers shaped like eyeballs lay tucked among other equally curious and macabre items on various shelves and tables.

As she predicted, Agatha found the real treasures in the third and fourth aisles. These items put a chill through her body and goosebumps on her arms. She liked to call the fourth aisle "Red Rum Row" because of the especially frightening items she sometimes found there. A few years earlier, Agatha had discovered the word 'murder' spelled backward was 'red rum.' She thought she'd been pretty clever naming the fourth aisle until she saw the movie *The Shining* and realized Stephen King had thought of it first.

Today's spine-chilling collection down Red Rum Row included a porcelain clown doll missing an eye. Its hand extended outward, holding a yellow balloon. An old book cover—minus the book—made of burgundy cloth embroidered with tiny flowers and titled *Flowers for my Dead Darling*. A clear glass canister with the label "Unheard Whispers." A faceless mannequin with no arms. A ceramic skeleton hanging upside down in a jar, its feet tied together, arms crisscrossed over its chest. And lastly, a wooden box with the words "DON'T OPEN ME" burned into the top.

"Whatcha think of that?" Agatha hadn't noticed her aunt behind her. Aunt Hattie was so small and slight she rarely made a sound when she walked.

"Why would it say, 'don't open me'?" She reached out and ran her fingers along the lettering on the top.

Aunt Hattie smiled. "It's a puzzle box. If you opened it, it would fall to pieces. And then you'd have to figure out how to put it back together again. That's the fun of it." She placed it in Agatha's hands. "Surprisingly heavy, isn't it?"

Agatha's eyes widened. The box was no larger than a bar of soap, but she nearly needed both hands to hold it. "Why is it like that?"

Aunt Hattie winked. "It must have many secrets."

Agatha turned the box over in her hands. Nothing was written or stamped on the bottom. She held it to her nose—she loved to smell things—and inhaled what she perceived to be burned wood, probably from the lettering etched on the top. It reminded her of a campfire. Something else was there, too, though. Something not so pleasant. A sourness of a sort. She wondered if the box had ever gotten wet.

"Is this new?"

Aunt Hattie hesitated. "Well, nothing in the shop is new, Agatha. Everything here is quite old and has a history and story to tell. Oh, if these things could only talk!"

Just then, the back door of the shop swung open, and, in the doorway, stood Mr. Dominicus, Aunt Hattie's only employee for the last five years. Mr. Dominicus reminded Agatha of a lumberjack because of his tall frame and broad, muscular shoulders, and he always wore plaid, flannel shirts. Two ice blue eyes were set in a manly face framed by a mustache and a beard braided to a point.

Mr. Dominicus lumbered when he walked, slightly dragging one leg behind him. His shoulders stooped over in a way that suggested he carried a certain amount of sadness upon them. Agatha didn't miss anything. Mr. Dominicus was helpful, friendly, and always ready with a welcoming smile. But something existed beneath the friendly face and greeting, a layer of unhappiness and sorrow. Agatha once asked Aunt Hattie about it. Her aunt explained Mr. Dominicus had been in some type of accident years ago, but she didn't know anything more.

Mr. Dominicus nodded when he saw Agatha. Royal blue and hunter green with a hint of white appeared to be today's choice of flannel, his braided beard secured with a matching blue rubber band.

"Well, good afternoon, Ms. Agatha." He smiled, a sheepish close-mouthed sort of grin showing no teeth.

"Hi," she said, still turning the puzzle box over in her hands again.

"Is this yours?" He called to Aunt Hattie as he shut the door and came inside.

"Hmm?" Aunt Hattie looked up from the booth where she was re-arranging the canister full of unheard whispers and the one-eyed clown doll who now lost the other eye as she moved it.

He held out a small white jar, its knob on top the shape of a black skull with wings. A simple etching of a black tree on its side adorned the side of the jar. Its dead, leafless branches splayed in different directions as if reaching in desperation for something as it fell.

Mr. Dominicus set it on a nearby table, studying it. Agatha turned to see her aunt's eyes were wide, one eyebrow arched in surprise, her mouth hanging open in an 'O.'

"A skull jar," Aunt Hattie whispered.

Agatha's stomach did two small flips, and she backed away. "That's really weird, Aunt Hattie. Can't you just dump it in the garbage?"

Mr. Dominicus repeated his question. "Is it yours, Hattie?" He looked from Agatha to Hattie and back again, confusion spreading over his face. "Should I throw it away?"

"No, just leave it there, Dom." Aunt Hattie, now recovered from her surprise, smiled. "Someone must have left it on the back steps as a do-nation. Sometimes people do that, thinking this place is a thrift shop." She gave a little laugh that wasn't a laugh at all. "Can you unload the four boxes I have in the storeroom for me while I take Agatha up front?"

Mr. Dominicus stroked his braided beard, ensuring the blue rubber band was still there. "Sure thing, Ms. Hattie."

She grabbed Agatha's hand and changed the subject, steering her toward her big oak desk. "I have something for you."

"For me?" Agatha loved presents.

"Of course. You think I forgot what tomorrow is?"

"I know you'd never forget, Aunt Hattie." Aunt Hattie's presents were her favorite because of their uniqueness. For her tenth birthday, Aunt Hattie wrapped a box of cookies-and-cream Pop-tarts. Agatha wasn't allowed much sugar at home, so the Pop-tarts were an extra special treat. She got a vintage feather boa and a silver frog ring for her eleventh birthday. For her twelfth, three rubber pencils bent in every direction, a container of slime, and two bracelets made of bones. And now, on the eve of birthday number thirteen, Agatha felt incredibly excited for what the next year would hold. After all, thirteen was a lucky number for Agatha.

"Is it the box?" Agatha said, giggling as they reached the desk. Aunt Hattie stopped. "Absolutely not."

Agatha's smile fell from her face. She was referring to a decorative, golden box that had been on her aunt's desk forever, probably even before Agatha was born. Over the years, Agatha had often asked her aunt to either touch it, open it, feel it, or smell it, among many other things. All her requests were met with the same twelve-word answer, which her aunt was repeating now:

"Someday, you'll need this, and someday it'll be yours. But not today." Aunt Hattie pushed the box from Agatha's view, shaking her head.

"First, let's start with an old favorite," Aunt Hattie continued. She opened the bottom drawer, her 'goody drawer,' as Agatha called it since it housed a variety of snacks, and pulled out a small package wrapped all in black with a bright orange ribbon crisscrossed over the front. Halloween colors, Agatha thought. Her favorite.

Agatha tore into the package, finding three stacked packs of black licorice Twizzlers, one on top of the other. She squealed with delight. Of everyone in the family, only she and Aunt Hattie liked the flavor. It was a funny thing, black licorice. One either loved it or hated it, and this was their special shared treat. And Aunt Hattie had shared a secret years ago: black licorice tasted best when stored in the freezer.

"Thank you, Auntie," Agatha said, giving Aunt Hattie a hug.

"I have one more thing, Agatha. Quite unexpectedly. Stay here for a moment." Her aunt hesitated but then pulled away, heading back down Red Rum Row, where they were just moments before.

When she returned, her hands were behind her back, a weird excitement painted across her face.

Agatha tore open one of the licorice bags, jamming half a Twizzler in her mouth until one cheek puffed out. She raised her eyebrows impatiently at her aunt. "Show me!" she giggled in between exaggerated chomps of the licorice.

Aunt Hattie bit her lip. "I've been waiting for this moment for a long time but didn't think it would be today. Tomorrow, maybe. Sometime this year, most likely. But not today." She slowly took both hands from behind her back to reveal the same little white jar with the fallen tree branch drawing Mr. Dominicus found outside only minutes before. She set it gently on the desk as if not wanting to disturb its contents.

Aunt Hattie grabbed the licorice bag from Agatha's hand, setting it out of the way, and held Agatha's hand uncomfortably tight. Her eyes motioned toward the jar. "Apparently, this is for you."

Agatha swallowed a portion of licorice far too large. She swallowed a second time, harder, to get it all down.

"What...what is it?" Agatha wasn't sure she wanted the answer.

Aunt Hattie put her blue-rimmed glasses back on her nose, her eyes magnified behind the lenses like a goldfish. "Your first ghost."

CHAPTER 3
CAKE AND AN EXPLANATION

For the second time that day, Agatha felt like running from an uncomfortable situation. But she planted both of her heels on the floor, pretending a cinderblock rested on top of each of her muddy shoes. She felt the bony fingers of unease dancing their way around her body again, this time counting her ribs, working their way upwards until they stopped at her collar bone and gently brushed her throat. She felt the need to gnaw a finger but kept her hands at her sides.

Aunt Hattie seemed extremely pleased with herself. She bit her lip, her hands clasped in front of her, awaiting Agatha's reply, attempting to contain thirteen years' worth of pent-up excitement.

Agatha finally managed a single word. "What?"

"Your first ghost!" Aunt Hattie exclaimed, this time much louder than before, a tsunami of words exiting her mouth as she finally unearthed a long-held secret that seemed to exhaust her.

She stood breathless before Agatha and tried to hand her the little jar.

"I don't want to touch it." Agatha doubted the truth of her own words. She very much wanted to touch it, to know what was inside, what history the jar held, and why it was 'hers' as Aunt Hattie had suggested. And was there a ghost inside of it? She jammed her left thumb into her mouth and bit down with the pointy end of her canine tooth. The thumbs were her favorite.

"Hattie, I'm finished. You only had two boxes in the back, not four." Mr. Dominicus suddenly appeared next to Aunt Hattie's desk. Agatha wondered how she hadn't heard him. Mr. Dominicus was not light-footed. His six-foot-five frame forced him to walk with an uneven gait that was nearly a stomp, one foot slightly heavier than the rest. There was no way he could ever sneak up on anybody, but today, somehow, he had.

"Do you want me to go ahead and vacuum before I leave? I don't mind." He pointed a thick meaty finger toward the back of the store.

Aunt Hattie set the jar back on her desk. "No, Dom. Actually, I think I might close early today. Tomorrow is Agatha's birthday, and I'm probably going to take her to dinner. So, go on and head home. I will see you tomorrow."

She walked with him to the store's back exit, too happy to be getting rid of him. She held the back door open, watching him walk down the road, making sure he was indeed leaving, waving and smiling as he disappeared around the nearest corner, heading toward the direction from which Agatha had come. That was another thing of interest to Agatha. Why didn't Mr. Dominicus drive? She'd never seen him in a car of any sort. Perhaps he lived near the store. She made a mental note to ask Aunt Hattie later.

Once her aunt was sure Mr. Dominicus was gone, Aunt Hattie rushed to the front of the store and turned off the OPEN sign,

taking care to secure five locks on the front door. Two chains, two deadbolts, and one latch that required an actual padlock. The number of locks seemed totally unnecessary, and she made another mental note for her aunt.

Aunt Hattie flipped off two switches that controlled the store's overhead lights, and everything was suddenly dark. One lone streetlamp from outside shone into the windows at the front of the store, but Agatha had to blink several times, letting her eyes adjust. Somehow, Aunt Hattie found Agatha's hand in the dark, taking the lead down Red Rum Row and out the back door of the store where Aunt Hattie's truck was waiting. Her aunt locked the handle and deadbolt of the back door and pulled two padlocks from her purse, putting them both on the door, tugging at each of them two to three times to ensure they were secure. Agatha was bewildered and couldn't hold on to her mental note any longer.

"Why so many locks?"

Aunt Hattie stopped tugging at the second padlock and paused as if searching for the most appropriate words to say. "Let's just say Dom comes back sometimes. At night. I don't like him in the store when I'm not here."

Do you need nine locks for Mr. Dominicus? Agatha thought but dared not say.

"Well, what about the mirror, then?" Agatha was in a questioning mood, and she pointed to the large mirror affixed to the outside of the back door.

Again, her aunt paused. "Miz Magnolia, a lady always checks her makeup and her teeth before being in the company of other people. Whether that be work, a social event, or taking their niece out on their birthday," she said in an exaggerated southern accent. "Before I open the shop for the day, Miz Honeysuckle checks her face like a good southern belle."

"But there's one on the front door, too," Agatha said.

Aunt Hattie gave the first padlock one last tug and, smiling, turned to her niece, ignoring her remark. "We'll go to my house and have a chat there. Along with something sweet. I'll call your father and tell him you'll be with me for a bit."

Aunt Hattie unlocked her truck and climbed into the driver's seat, sitting on a pillow so she could see over the dashboard. *A grey-haired child behind the steering wheel*, Agatha thought. In her right hand was the little jar from inside the store. Aunt Hattie had made a point not to leave it behind.

They drove the twenty-five minutes to Aunt Hattie's house in silence. Agatha wondered why her aunt didn't live closer to her store. She lived in Gulfport, the neighboring city to Biloxi, and it wasn't an easy drive. There were about forty-seven turns Aunt Hattie took just to get back to her little two-room house out in the middle of nowhere. Aunt Hattie had no neighbors, and Agatha knew she liked it that way.

The only visitors were the three white cats who practically lived with her aunt, each with a single black mark of some sort on their chest. They'd prowl the land surrounding the house, keeping watch for Aunt Hattie, who was their keeper, spoiling them nightly with dried kibble and warm milk. Aunt Hattie went to great lengths to make sure the cats were taken care of. Warm in the winter. Cool in the summer. Happy and content.

Agatha lurched forward as Aunt Hattie threw the truck into park. Her seatbelt tightened against her chest, and Agatha sighed in exasperation. "Aunt Hattie," she began, but her aunt was already up the stairs on the front porch. She watched her in disbelief through the cracked and dirty windshield. Why was she so excited?

"Well, come on!" Aunt Hattie stamped her foot twice with a smile on her face. "I'll make ya some noodles."

"Noodles" to Aunt Hattie wasn't spaghetti noodles or linguine or fettuccine or any type of pasta. What she meant by "noodles" was Aunt Hattie's signature dish: green peas and mushroom soup mixed together and poured over crispy, crunchy dried Chinese Chun-King noodles. It looked like dog food and tasted like Heaven. And Agatha loved it.

Agatha unbuckled her seatbelt and shook her head as she entered Aunt Hattie's modest kitchen: one small dining room table with two chairs in the center of the small room. A few brown cabinets. A dirty microwave on the counter. An old, yellow refrigerator hummed a low, monotone song of one long, never-ending note while Aunt Hattie set the small jar from the store in the middle of the wooden dining room table.

Her aunt set to work throwing two cans of peas and one can of mushroom soup into a scratched, silver pan on top of the stove, grabbing two bowls with blue flowers etched in the center of them from one of the cabinets, whistling a sweet, happy tune as the mushroom soup mixture popped and sizzled over the stove's blue flame. She opened the round tin of Chinese noodles, dumping them in the bowls until the blue flowers were covered with what looked like a dead forest of dried sticks.

She set the two bowls on the table and, with a smile, presented Agatha with a spoon.

"Enjoy, my love!" Her aunt giggled.

Agatha looked down at her dinner and bit her lip. She eyed the jar, a few inches away from her bowl. Aunt Hattie broke her thoughts.

"I've been preparing for this conversation for a very long time, and now that it's here, I'm not quite sure what to say." She exhaled a nervous laugh and removed her glasses from her face, letting them dangle by their multicolored chain against her navy dress.

"Is there a ghost in the jar?" Agatha interrupted, hoping to move the conversation along.

Hattie shook her head. "No, no ghost in the jar, dear. Most likely, it is some sort of contact or clue."

"A clue for what?"

Her aunt paused, watching Agatha twirl her spoon in a pile of peas. "For a ghost that needs something. Or wants something. Sometimes we don't know which."

Agatha jerked her head up. "We?"

"Yes. We." Aunt Hattie clasped her hands in front of her and took a breath. "I can see them too."

"Ghosts?"

Her aunt nodded.

"What do you mean 'too'? I don't see ghosts." Agatha set down her spoon too quickly, and a slosh of mushroom soup splattered over the side of her bowl.

Aunt Hattie's face softened as she grabbed a paper towel. "Of course, you do, dear. You just haven't realized it all these years. In fact, I've seen you do it. There are ghosts all around us, occupying the negative space—that void between life and the afterlife, if you will—and most of us go about our daily lives never seeing them. But there are a few of us—Perceivers, we call them— who see them and interact with them. Sometimes we even befriend them!" Aunt Hattie chuckled.

"Perceiver?" Agatha kept her eyes on her aunt.

"Yes. We are Perceivers, Agatha. We see things. We know things. We solve things."

"What ghosts have you seen me talk to?" Agatha asked. Now she was concerned.

"Well, Big, for one."

Big? Agatha thought. Big had been her imaginary friend a few years ago when she was in elementary school. He'd looked like Alfred E. Neuman on the cover of Mad Magazine, with curly burnt orange hair, a button nose, and a gap between his two front teeth. Except, Big dressed fancily, Agatha remembered, usually in a tuxedo with no shoes. He'd been quiet, rarely saying anything but going along with whatever Agatha wanted to do on that particular day. When he did speak, he whispered his words in an English accent.

Her parents played along, too, setting an extra dish at the table for Big, making a mat with a pillow for Big on her floor at night, chalking it up to either the imagination or the loneliness of only children. Big was a part of the family until one day when her father asked her where Big was.

Agatha's reply had been prompt, short, and curt. "Big's dead." And that was that. Though Agatha had no recollection of what actually happened to Big, those were the words that came from

her mouth that day when she was about six.

Agatha shook off her mental picture of Big. "You saw Big, Aunt Hattie?"

Her aunt nodded her head. "I did." "Big was a ghost?"

"Most likely, yes. Most imaginary friends are ghosts."

"But you said ghosts. As in, plural. Who else have I talked to that's a ghost?"

Aunt Hattie brushed Agatha off. "We'll get to that. That is not important this evening. What IS important is this little jar. I received one just like it when I turned thirteen." Aunt Hattie was lost in a memory, and she bit the inside of her cheek, gnawing on it for a few seconds.

"Aunt Hattie?"

"Yes. Yes. Sorry. What was I saying? Oh yes. I received a jar just like this with the fallen tree on the side of it as my first 'case,' if you will. The skull jar is always a ghost's first contact. Mine ended up being a ghost that needed help finding her missing wedding ring, of all things.

Someone had stolen it during her wake. Can you believe that? Either way, that's how I knew this one was for you, of course. The fallen tree on the side and all. I recognized it immediately. Fallen trees are a symbol of mortality. Death, I mean to say. Did you know that? I bet you didn't. Learn something new every day!" Aunt Hattie was out of breath.

Agatha waited a few seconds. "But how did you know it was for me?"

"Perceivers run in families. Usually, it skips a generation or even two, but not always. You've exhibited all the qualities of a Perceiver, coupled with the ghosts I know you've seen. So, I just knew."

"What qualities?"

Aunt Hattie got up from her chair and took Agatha's bowl from her, still full of noodles, and scraped it off in the garbage. "Most Perceivers are nervous types. They exhibit some sort of worried or scared, or nervous quality. For me, I gnaw the inside of my cheek. For you, you bite your nails." Aunt Hattie gently washed the bowl in the sink, her back to Agatha. "That will never stop, by the way. The nail-biting."

Agatha snorted. "Tell mom and dad that."

"I wish I could, but this will have to stay between you and me. Those who do not have the gift or those who are not Perceivers will never understand." Her aunt was now digging deep into the refrigerator, her glasses back on the end of her nose, rummaging and moving items around until she found what she wanted: a small vanilla cake frosted in white with two small pink flowers on top. "And not everyone who sees ghosts are Perceivers. Some people see apparitions haunting old buildings or ghosts of their family members, but that doesn't mean they'll get assignments. Being a Perceiver is very special."

Frowning, she set the cake on the table in front of Agatha. "I know it's complicated. Here, you'd rather eat this than the noodles, I know. It's your birthday tomorrow, so do what you like! Also, I'm sorry about the flowers. Nobody makes black flowers."

Agatha hated pink but didn't mind this time. She immediately picked one flower off the cake and popped the whole thing in her mouth at once.

Aunt Hattie was once again seated across from Agatha. This time, she reached for her niece's hand. Agatha licked her fingers and set one hand in the palm of her aunt's. "I also knew you were a Perceiver because you like black licorice. Not all people who eat black licorice are Perceivers, but all Perceivers like black licorice. Honestly, I'd say ninety-nine percent of people hate black licorice, and you and I are the only ones in the family who like it. Well, I take that back. Uncle Tim did."

With her free hand, Aunt Hattie fingered a necklace she always wore, rubbing the silver spiral dangling from a silver chain.

Agatha felt her aunt's fingers tighten around hers. Uncle Tim was the uncle who'd died in the war, whose grave was on Agatha's way home. Most family members didn't speak his name. He was this silent, sad cloud that sometimes hung around family gatherings. You knew it was there, dark and lovely, brooding in the corner, heavy with the weight of its own sadness. But no one wanted to talk about it. So much so that Agatha hardly knew anything about him except what she'd learned from Aunt Hattie, who wasn't afraid to mention his name now and then.

"He was a Perceiver, too?" Agatha asked.

Hattie shook her head. "You know, I'm not sure. I never got the chance to ask him. He died when he was eighteen, so we never had that conversation." She looked down at her necklace. "This was his, you know. The only thing I have of his." She held the silver spiral up for Agatha to view.

"I never take it off. I haven't since the day my mother gave it to me. After he was killed. It's probably the most important thing I own." Her aunt loosened her grip and put her other hand over the top of Agatha's until her small hand was a sandwich of bitten fingers between her aunt's silky palms.

"Agatha, we share the same gift. I can guide you, but I cannot help you. The ghosts that come to you are your own, not mine. Sometimes they need nothing more than a kind word or a gentle reminder to lay back down and sleep if you understand what I mean. But that is rare. Usually, they want more. The dead usually contact the living when they need assistance with something. Something they can't do or solve on their own. And they only contact a Perceiver. Not that they can tell you. You'll have to figure out what it is they want."

A wave of seriousness washed over her aunt's face. "I will admit that not all ghosts are friendly. There will be forces against you. Forces that don't want you to succeed. Forces that don't want the dead to get their help."

Agatha was suddenly interested. "What kind of forces?"

Aunt Hattie arched one eyebrow upward, followed by the corner of her mouth in the same direction. "You never know. It's always different. Sometimes it's a chill up your spine, an unseen hand on your shoulder that won't go away, a warning whispered on the leaves of trees, or a bad feeling when you turn a corner. Mostly, it takes the shape of a person. Someone or something doing the evil work of the evil dead. Deceivers, they're called. And make no mistake, they will try to undo or keep you from doing what you're doing. The most important thing is to stay the course."

Agatha tried to swallow. She tasted the cake, but it was no longer sweet. It came up the back of her throat in the form of a burp and was mixed with bits of black licorice and the hot dog she'd had for lunch. She wanted to gag.

Aunt Hattie patted Agatha's hand twice and smiled. "But never mind about that." She plucked the second pink flower from the cake and, before crushing it between her teeth, said, "You must be strong, Agatha. You have all the gifts you need to succeed. Have courage in your heart. It's a very powerful thing to be a Perceiver."

CHAPTER 4
THE CLOSET MONSTER

After their shared cake, Aunt Hattie dropped Agatha off at home, but not before putting her finger to her lips, reminding Agatha to be quiet about their conversation.

Her aunt's truck sputtered away as Agatha climbed the three steps to the modest Anxious family home. Built in 1928, it was situated on Azalea Drive near the beach, where traffic roared by at all hours of the night.

The Anxious house had three tiny bedrooms, only one of which was empty and used as her mother's sewing room where she didn't sew pockets. One large room that made up the dining room and living room was at the front of the house, and a small bathroom all three members of the Anxious family shared was sandwiched between the bedrooms. Most days, Agatha was thankful to be an only child, considering how much time her father took in the bathroom, reading on the toilet.

A small kitchen was at the back of the house and was usually where Agatha could find her mother, Anita Anxious, trying different home-made and invented 'recipes,' her hair in a messy blonde bun, an apron tied around her thin frame, oversized brown glasses swallowing her face. Two or three straight pins were sometimes clenched between her teeth as she tried to cook and sew simultaneously, a hazardous hobby Agatha's father often demanded his wife quit.

Agatha turned the scratched brass knob and opened the front door, making a beeline straight to her room, the skull jar tucked tightly in the corner of her bookbag by Aunt Hattie. Agatha still hadn't touched it. The family's black German Shepherd, Macbeth, was stretched across Agatha's bed as if it were his own.

Her mother appeared in her doorway, wearing an apron with winking apples on it. "Good day at school, Agatha?"

"Sure."

Anita Anxious was tucking a straight pin into one of the pockets of her apron. "Any tests or quizzes?"

"No." Lately, she answered her mother in short, one-word responses, but her mother took no offense, chalking it up to 'those teen years,' she would sometimes say.

Her mother smiled. "Ok, well, dinner will be ready in an hour.

Dad won't be home until tomorrow."

Agatha nodded, working on her thumb with her front teeth, deciding not to tell her mother she'd already had two pieces of cake.

Agatha's dad, Sonny—whose real name was Virgil, but he hated that name, and nobody called him that unless they were trying to get on his nerves—worked at one of the seafood canning factories on the beach in Biloxi. An area locals called The Point, right near the foot of the bridge that connected Biloxi to the neighboring city of Ocean Springs.

About fifty percent of the time, his job required him to work days. The other fifty percent of the time, he worked overnight. And one hundred percent of the time, he came home smelling like fish. Agatha always thought he smelled a bit like cat food, too, but that was just her opinion.

When the dinner she didn't eat was over, and her nightly routine of dishes, bath, and homework was complete, Agatha placed a small music box against her closet door to keep in the closet monster, whom she imagined lived between her clothes. Yawning, she crept into her soft, worn sheets. She'd gone to say goodnight to her mother but found her fast asleep on the couch, swatches of different fabric still in her left hand.

As Agatha lay flat on her back in the darkness of her room, an avocado-sized ball of nerves settled in her stomach. She didn't like being awake when her parents were asleep. Her mouth felt dry, and she rolled onto her side. She wished her father was home.

Agatha's dad wasn't a large man, but he was powerful in his own right, muscles lining his calves, stomach, arms, and either side of his long neck. His job required long hours and heavy lifting, but the size of his muscles didn't outweigh the size of his kind heart. His muscles also paled in comparison to the size of his hair. His tight, black curls encircled his head like a helmet and resembled an afro.

After what seemed like an hour, Agatha crawled out of bed, letting her eyes adjust to the darkness before tip-toeing across the wooden floor in the hall toward the bathroom. Having spent her entire life in the same house, she knew all the areas of the creaking floor to avoid. She turned on the nightlight next to the sink and bent her head underneath the faucet, strands of her wavy blonde hair falling into the sink. The water from the bathroom sink tastes so much better than the water from the kitchen sink, Agatha thought as it poured into her mouth, cool against her tongue. She gulped until her small belly was full.

She was wiping her mouth on the brown hand towel, thinking how much it smelled like a wet dog, when she saw, reflected in the mirror in front of her, her closet door open. Agatha's left thumb immediately found its way to her open mouth as she inched toward her bedroom. She nibbled for a few minutes as she stood in her doorway, wide-eyed, staring at her closet, its door ever so slightly ajar, the wooden music box pushed away from the door about an inch.

"Mom!" she said in the loudest whisper she could manage. There was no answer. "Mommy!" she said again, more urgently this time. She hadn't called her mother that in a very long time. Suddenly, she heard Aunt Hattie's voice from earlier. Have courage in your heart. It is a very powerful thing to be a Perceiver.

She swallowed hard and stepped into her room, walking slowly and silently as if not to alert the closet monster of her presence. Once in front of the closet, she quietly pressed her hand to the door until it was closed and put her desk chair in front of it. Perhaps the music box wasn't heavy enough to keep the door closed. Maybe Macbeth had brushed past the door and pushed the small box out of the way. Agatha tried to invent other excuses to make herself feel less afraid.

Agatha climbed back into bed, crossed her hands over her chest, and took a deep breath, something she often did when she was afraid. Generally, Agatha felt that oxygen was the best form of medicine for her worries. After five deep breaths-Agatha liked odd numbers for everything-she turned on the lamp beside her bed.

It was only when the soft yellow light filled the room that she noticed the small white jar on her desk.

Someone had set it out.

Agatha crept past her sleeping mother on her tiptoes toward the kitchen where her cell phone was charging. An old, refurbished flip phone without any of the bells and whistles had been an early birthday gift from her parents. It was cracked in places, but it worked, and Agatha had been excited to receive it.

She dialed Aunt Hattie's number. On the third ring, her aunt picked up.

"Yes, love?"

"Aunt Ha-ha-attie," Agatha stammered. "The jar!" It was all Agatha could manage in a low whisper so as not to rouse her mother.

"What about it?"

Agatha tried to think of the right words to say, but her mind was foggy with fear. "It's out of my backpack. Somehow. Someone...It's sitting on my desk!"

Her aunt's voice was now firm. "Agatha, listen to me. You have to open the jar. You can't ignore it, and it won't just go away, my dear. It wants to be opened."

Aunt Hattie paused before uttering, "Remember what I said about not being afraid." And then her aunt hung up.

Agatha held her breath as she walked toward her bedroom, peering in slowly as if expecting to see someone or something sitting on her bed. Her room was empty. Even the closet door was still closed. Her eyes glanced toward her desk, where the little white jar still sat, and Agatha took note of how innocent it looked. Innocent in its simplicity. White. Small. Not scary at all.

It's what's inside that's scary, Agatha thought to herself. Her left hand held her right, a middle finger picking at the other middle finger's cuticle. Back and forth. An argument of middle fingers. She inched her way toward the jar. On the way, she grabbed the chair from in front of the closet and placed it in front of her desk in its usual spot. She eased herself into it, her heart pounding a beat in her brain. Her ears pulsed with the rhythm.

She sat, staring at the jar until her lids got heavy and sleep beckoned her. Finally, with one deep sigh, she reached out and grabbed the small ceramic jar in her left hand. It was cool to the touch and very light as if it were made of paper. She held it away from her as she popped off the tiny lid with her right hand, half expecting a goblin or ghoul to spring forth from the jar, but nothing happened.

Agatha was surrounded by the silence of her bedroom. She turned the jar upside down, and a small, white, pristine, rolled-up piece of paper fell onto the desk. Agatha took the pointy end of a nearby pencil and tried to unroll the paper without touching it. Giving up, she finally grabbed the tiny piece between her fingers and unrolled it while she held her breath.

In the scribbled, childish handwriting of someone unused or unaccustomed to holding a pencil was one word:

CHAPTER 5
SHOW AND TELL

The next morning, a sleepy, red-eyed Agatha dragged herself into her first period: Mr. Barone's History class.

Mr. Barone, tall, slim, and balding on top, was seated behind his desk at the front of the classroom, scratching his temple with the eraser end of a pink pencil. He sipped a cup of coffee, raising an eyebrow when he saw Agatha.

"Good morning, Miss Anxious. Sleep well?" He tipped his coffee cup toward her, and she gave him a thumbs up. Agatha adored his sarcastic wit. Mr. Barone was one of the nicer teachers at Michel Middle School. He was always in a good mood and ready first thing in the morning with a smile or a joke, which Agatha attributed to the large cup of coffee he always had in his left hand. Mr. Barone was also one of the better-dressed teachers, usually in a pair of dress slacks, a long sleeve white collared shirt with a tie tucked neatly inside a sleeveless, colorful sweater. Today, a tie with lemon yellow stripes was expertly nestled inside a sweater of grape purple. It reminded Agatha of Mardi Gras.

Agatha settled into her desk, which was at the very end of the first row, the row nearest the door. When teachers allowed students to choose their own desks—a rarity—Agatha always chose the back of the classroom because it made her more comfortable. And always nearest the door. She liked to know her escape route should she ever need it. In thirteen years, she'd yet to need an escape route, but with the way things were shaping up recently, she felt she soon might.

She grabbed a grey notebook from her bookbag and placed it on her desk as Leopold Panic entered the room. He hadn't gotten to choose his seat like almost everyone else had. Mr. Barone used a hat to 'decide' all sorts of things, including each student's desk assignment. Leopold's name had been drawn last, and thus, he'd been stuck in the front of the classroom. Front and center, to be exact. A seat that made Agatha itch with unease.

Leopold avoided Agatha's eyes, and everyone else's for that matter, as he slipped quietly into his desk. He folded his arms in front of him, resting his forehead on them like a pillow.

"That kid is so weird." A deep voice boomed to Agatha's left.

Without looking, she knew it was Dorian Doom.

She wanted to ignore him but changed her mind. "YOU'RE weird." She stared straight ahead but could see him in her periphery. Agatha saw him smirk from the corner of her eye.

Never the one to keep his opinions to himself, Dorian held a bit of mystery for Agatha. A puzzle she had yet to put together. Sometimes he peered nervously from underneath the overhang of his monstrous eyebrows. His ice-blue eyes could wound with one stare. Agatha thought his eyes were cold, with a general lack of feeling. His brows were dark and full, giving Dorian a permanent glare, and Agatha could never tell whether Dorian was happy or angry. Although, he never seemed to be either. Mostly, he existed in a constant state of nothingness, neither happy nor sad nor, well, anything.

His voice.

Agatha had forgotten how deep it was. Like somebody on theradio calling football plays or giving bad news about a local car wreck. Probably the latter, she thought since he always seemed to be saying something negative or macabre. He sounded like he might be an interviewer on one of those crime shows her mother watched on Friday nights. She hated to admit she kind of liked it.

Mr. Barone's far higher voice cut through her thoughts. "Alright, well, good morning, ladies and gents. Happy Tuesday morning to all of you. Some of us look as though it isn't quite so happy, so let's see what we can do to change that, eh? I have a fun assignment you all will like this morning. Put your notebooks and pencils and everything away."

Agatha watched as students looked left and right at their neighbors, a curiosity spreading across their faces. Any assignment that did not require a book, paper, or pencil must be a fun one. She, as a general rule, however, preferred to neither be optimistic nor pessimistic. She liked to be realistic, and today, she had an inkling Mr. Barone's assignment would be the sort of fun only a teacher would find entertaining.

Mr. Barone soon confirmed Agatha's suspicions. "This is usually not a thing for History class, but it is a skill all of you will need out in the real world someday. It's also the number one fear of most humans. Can anybody tell me what that is?"

"Public speaking," Agatha said under her breath.

Mr. Barone was right. Everybody did hate public speaking, including Agatha, but she wouldn't have said it was her greatest fear. She feared small talk the most. The kind you do in the elevator while you're riding up thirty-five floors or at the grocery store while the bag boy is bagging your groceries. People just talked to fill up the weird space of silence that made them uncomfortable. What was wrong with silence anyway?

Mr. Barone chuckled. "Now, I doubt I'll have any volunteers, so I'll just call your names one by one. You'll each have one minute to tell me what you did last weekend. And as I'm sure Mrs. Wright has taught you, remember that a good speech has a beginning, a middle, and a conclusion. And just for good measure, add a joke of some sort in there. It's a great opener with your audience."

"Mrs. Wright has never taught us that." A black-haired girl named Tippy Trinkle piped up, gnawing ferociously on a piece of bubblegum. Tippy was always piping up about everything, sometimes inserting her opinion where it wasn't wanted and always when it wasn't asked for. Agatha found her amusing.

"And honestly, Mr. Barone, she doesn't teach us much at all." Tippy stared at Mr. Barone, awaiting a response.

Agatha had to agree. Mrs. Wright, the English teacher, was everything Mr. Barone was not: unhappy, rude, negative, impatient, and all the things that generally made her Mrs. Wrong instead of Mrs. Wright.

Mr. Barone took a sip from his mug and ignored her. "Leopold, how about you go first?"

Agatha's head shot up. Once again, it confirmed why Leopold's desk was in the worst possible location.

Leopold sighed and tucked his hair behind his ear as he reluctantly left his desk. Agatha had seen Leopold do the same movement with his hair at the cemetery, and he did it repeatedly as he walked to the front of the classroom, even though every hair was perfectly in place. He faced the class, his green eyes full of nerves as he scanned the curious, waiting faces.

Mr. Barone smiled. "Beginning, middle, and end. And don't forget the joke." He gently nudged Leopold with his words.

Leopold looked down, avoiding the sea of expectant eyeballs. His hand went to his ear again. "Like most weekends, I really did nothing. I don't have that many options, really. Biloxi is pretty boring. My weekends are about as empty as my father's head." He paused. One giggle came from Tippy.

Mr. Barone nodded. "Good," he whispered.

Leopold continued, eyes still on the floor. "It was pretty boring until I decided to head to the Old Biloxi Cemetery on Sunday. By myself." He looked up to see if he'd earned any respect for being in a cemetery by himself. Dorian yawned.

Leopold returned his gaze to the floor. "I stayed there for a while, listening to the wind. And then I left." He looked over at Mr. Barone. "The end," he finished.

Mr. Barone cleared his throat. "Well, alright, Leopold. Thank you for that simple but concise speech." He tucked his lips into his mouth into a false smile and nodded toward Leopold as if he'd expected nothing less than a half-hearted, strange, and vague story.

"Let's see, who's next? Hmmm," Mr. Barone pretended to think hard as he scanned the room of nervous students who avoided his gaze. One by one, he selected victims who trudged to the front of the classroom as slowly as possible, giving their one-minute play-by-play of what amounted to a classroom full of very boring weekends, Agatha thought. Mr. Barone did this until two remained: she and Dorian.

Mr. Barone smiled. "Today is Agatha's birthday, class, so I am excusing her from this assignment. Consider this my small token of a birthday present, Agatha." She smiled amidst the sound of three or four jealous groans. It was the perfect birthday present since she had no intention of telling anybody about the skull jar.

"So that only leaves you, Mr. Doom," Mr. Barone continued. "Please, enlighten us."

Dorian left his desk and walked to the front of the room with confidence Agatha took note of. He held his head high, unbothered by the assignment of public speaking. He cleared his throat and popped every knuckle on his left hand before he began, looking straight at Agatha as he spoke his speech's opening words. "Good morning, fellow classmates, and happy birthday,

Agatha."

She blushed.

His lips curled up on one side of his mouth into a sarcastic smile, and she saw how pointed his eye teeth were. "I went to Deer Island last weekend." He paused on purpose, allowing the silence in the room to be noticeable, the whirring of the metal ceiling fan the only sound.

"That's what I thought. Going to Deer Island isn't exactly an amazing time. Most of you have already been, and to be honest, it's too hot to be any fun. So, I know none of you are impressed, but I left with something I didn't have when I arrived."

He paused again, his right hand finding its way into his right pocket, turning something over and over in there. Agatha could see his knuckles working in several different directions. He stood, silent, the sarcastic smile now spread over his entire face.

"Well, come on. What is it?" Tippy interrupted, popping a bubble.

Dorian withdrew his hand from the pocket and held up a single gold coin. At first, Agatha wasn't sure what it was since she was seated at the back of the room. She squinted, and the item came into focus. It indeed looked like a coin, but it was imperfect as if it had been made by a novice or someone inexperienced and definitely long ago. She raised her eyebrows, wondering how much it was worth.

"It's solid gold and has a picture on the back, but I can't tell what it is because it's so old. This is probably worth a million dollars. So, in conclusion, I became a millionaire last weekend. The end."

Satisfied with himself, Dorian carefully placed the coin back in his pocket and slid back into his chair next to Agatha.

Mr. Barone set down his coffee cup and followed right behind him. "Care to pass it around, Mr. Doom? That is quite an interesting find."

Dorian stared flatly at him. "I'd rather not."

"Alright, well, then how about sharing it with just your history teacher?" Mr. Barone held out his hand.

Dorian rolled his eyes and placed the coin in Mr. Barone's waiting palm. Agatha could see it was larger than a regular coin. Flat and uneven, like she'd seen from afar. There were numerals and a picture of some sort, just like Dorian said.

"Where did you find this?" Mr. Barone asked. "On Deer Island."

Mr. Barone huffed. "I know that, Dorian. Where on Deer Island? Be specific."

Dorian, surprised at his teacher's impatience, quickly answered. "I...I don't know. Like, heading to the water's edge. There's a large area of brush and trees and bushes before the shore. I stepped on it in there, right before we got back in our boat."

"And you decided to take it?"

Dorian snickered. "Why wouldn't I? It's probably worth something."

Just then, the bell rang. Mr. Barone handed the coin back, pressing it heavily into Dorian's hand. A little too hard, Agatha thought.

The bell tolled loudly in the background, with an urgency as most of their classmates gathered their bags and books, eager for break or gym or whatever the next hour held for them. Agatha packed her backpack at a turtle's pace, hoping to catch what Mr. Barone was saying to Dorian. Their conversation had an unfinished air. She purposely dropped her pencil between the desks.

Mr. Barone still held two fingers on the coin as he pressed it harder into his pupil's hand. "I just hope some sort of misfortune doesn't befall you, Mr. Doom. I'm a big believer that people don't just get lucky, you know. It's usually some sort of test, and if that is the case, you've failed. It's called karma. Look it up."

CHAPTER 6
A MESSAGE IN THE DARKNESS

That evening, Agatha tossed and turned on her stiff little twin bed, throwing aside pillows that were either too flat, too fat, or too fluffy. The air was muggy with the

Mississippi humidity. A heavy stickiness coated the room, leaving small beads of sweat on her arms and neck. She wiped them away with her hand, deciding to lick her fingers and taste the saltiness.

The house had two air conditioner units, neither of which were in Agatha's room. Both were situated in window frames, unsteady and unstable as if they might tumble out of the window at any given moment. One wonky unit sat in the dining room window like a lopsided pig, drooling and keeping watch over food on the nightly dinner table, overgrown and smushed into a space too small for all of its parts. Agatha, who had nicknames for just about everything, called this air conditioning unit Porkchop Cupcake. Most of the time, Porkchop Cupcake wasn't even on since no one in the Anxious family liked cold air being blown full force on them as they ate.

The other unit, affectionately known as Taco Chubs—also fat and overgrown and also named by Agatha—was, of course, in her parents' room, constantly on and blowing full blast. At night, they kept their door closed, hogging all of the cold air, something about which Agatha continuously whined, but her complaints were often ignored.

Tonight, Agatha lay face up, eyes toward the ceiling, wondering what time it was as a crack of lightning lit up her room. The winds outside her bedroom were unhappy, whipping past her window with a purpose through the trees in her backyard, rattling the tubes of the wind chimes her mother kept on the back patio. They moaned with each gust of wind, each groan louder and stronger than the last as if they longed to be percussion instruments but knew they had no chance.

Agatha grabbed a small chunk of her hair, smoothed it between her fingers as she divided the strands into three sections, and set about pulling the hair tight in a perfect braid. She then placed the braid under her nose, puckered her lips, and pretended she had a mustache. She stroked the braid with her eyes closed, a methodical movement that sometimes put her to sleep. But not this night.

Another crack of lightning was followed by a loud boom of thunder. Agatha smiled. She didn't mind. She loved a good storm. While other kids her age were asking to snuggle with their parents during bad weather, Agatha wished she were out in it, letting the rain pelt her face as she looked up to the sky.

She flung a sweaty arm over the side of the bed, reaching down to find Macbeth where he always slept. She let her hand rest on his stomach. He breathed heavily. A twitch of his body here and there told Agatha he was in the middle of a dream. She wondered whether it was bad or good.

Suddenly, he let out a small snarl, so low and quiet that Agatha wasn't sure she'd heard correctly. Then it came again, this time from deep in his belly. Her hand vibrated with the growl, and she snatched it away. Macbeth never growled. Agatha often said his heart was made of marshmallows.

"Mac!" she called to him, leaning over the bed and clapping her hands a couple of times, trying to rouse him from his nightmare. It was only as she leaned closer and her eyes adjusted to the dark that she discovered he wasn't lying down at all. In fact, he was now at attention, on all fours, ready to pounce on something in the corner. She saw his teeth were showing, and strings of saliva hung from his lips, but he didn't move. She reluctantly followed his gaze toward the far corner of her room near her closet door. Thankfully, the door was shut, but the corner right near the closet where her desk was seemed unusually dark, even with the occasional flash of lightning.

She squinted, and her eyes adjusted more. She could make out lumps and bumps and jagged figures, but nothing looked like a person.

Why in the world would there be a person in your room, Agatha? she asked herself. She'd double-checked under her bed and triple-checked her closet before bedtime. She knew her conversation with Aunt Hattie the previous day had something to do with it. But Aunt Hattie said she had to find the ghost, didn't she? Or did she? She couldn't remember exactly. She tore a small bit of skin from her left middle finger and rolled it around in her mouth.

Macbeth interrupted her thoughts with another snarl.

"That is enough, Mac!" Agatha said in a huff, throwing off her damp sheets and standing with determination. "I am not afraid," she announced aloud. She inched toward her desk with false courage, her hands in front of her to keep her from bumping into anything, her heart drumming a solo of fear. Her fingers found the desk chair, and she slowly ran them across the desk toward the wall. She spread out her arms left and right in a breaststroke of air, finding nothing.

She sighed. "Exactly. What's your problem?" She faced Macbeth. "Dumb dog."

Turning back toward the desk, she ran her hands across all the objects on top of it, items that formed the jagged-shaped silhouettes she'd seen earlier. Books, two trophies from elementary school spelling bees, a jewelry box, two decks of cards, a slinky, a cup full of markers, a few shells from trips to the beach, and half a sand dollar. She held the last item, admiring its chalky smoothness between her fingers, trying to fully see it in the darkness.

She let out a snort. In thirteen years, she'd never found a full sand dollar on the beach, but that didn't mean she hadn't tried. They were always broken or halved by the time Agatha got her hands on one.

She threw the sand dollar back on the desk, but when she did, it hit something plastic and made a rattling noise somewhat familiar to Agatha. She reached out her hands again until her hands touched the plastic. Her fingers felt the small grooves. She traced the lines until they formed squares, one after the other. It was her Scrabble board, open on her desk, and the tiles were scattered around it.

She didn't recall leaving it out. In fact, she wouldn't leave it out. Macbeth was known to chew small items, mostly things of importance to Agatha, and she always put away her games when she was done playing them. Not that she'd even played Scrabble recently.

In the dark, her hands found her desk lamp. She yanked the cord a little too hard, and the small grey lamp toppled over. Setting it upright, she began to gather the little wooden tiles slipping them back into the purple velvet bag she used to hold the pieces. It was only as she gathered her third handful of tiles that she realized why the tiles were out in the first place.

There, neatly across the center star on the Scrabble board, as if someone had played their first turn, were several small words jammed into one:

CHAPTER 7
THE SAD AND LONELY GRAVE

The following morning, Agatha was already awake when her alarm clock went off at 6:07 a.m. She tapped it as quickly as she could and covered up her head with her blanket, her breath filling the small, enclosed space under the sheets.

When she could stand it no more, she pulled the sheets down from her face, an inch at a time, until only her eyes were visible. From her bed, she stared at the Scrabble board on her desk. She could not read the words, but she could tell the letters were still there, all twelve of them, in the center of the board.

"Mom!" she called, motionless.

Her mother soon appeared in her doorway, a toothbrush in the left corner of her mouth. "Yes, honey? Oh, you're not going to be late, are you? Come on and get up."

"I don't feel good," Agatha managed in the most pitiful voice she could muster. It was barely a whisper, as if her throat was raw and sore. It was the only affliction she could think of. Sore throats were usually her go-to fib when she felt like she wanted to stay home from school.

Mrs. Anxious gave her daughter a frown, cocking her head to one side as if deciding something.

"Wait. Mom, are you going somewhere?"

"Sorry. I thought I told you. I'm training a lady today during the brunch shift. She usually works nights. Penny something. Can't remember her last name." Her mother worked part-time waitressing tables at The Pearly Oyster, a seafood restaurant on the beach, famous for its raw, slimy oysters on the half shell, which, surprisingly, Agatha liked.

"Uggghhhhh," Agatha groaned, throwing off her covers with a huff, being careful to exit the side of the bed farthest from her desk. "I'll just go to school."

"I don't mind if you want to stay home, hon. I just won't be here for a bit."

"No. Forget it, Mom. I'm fine," she said, giving a couple of loud coughs for her mother to hear. She'd rather go to school than be left alone in the house.

Agatha inched her way around her room, back to the wall, moving slowly toward her closet. She avoided looking at the Scrabble board, which she felt had grown eyes over the dark hours of the night and now seemed to stare at her, willing her to look at its wooden face. She pulled a black dress from its hanger, removed her nightgown, and slipped the dress over her head, her blonde hair pointing in all directions with a wiry stiffness. She pulled on a pair of dark grey stockings and grabbed her backpack.

She turned to find Macbeth sitting in her doorway, his large brown eyes fully open in investigation mode. She tried to call him to her, but he refused.

"Bye, Mom. Love you," she said as she slammed the back door, not waiting for her mother's reply. Her stomach growled twice as she walked toward the school. She'd skipped breakfast and was regretting it.

She cut through Biloxi Cemetery in a rush, seeing the graves in her side view, but ignoring them. She had a feeling Leopold might be waiting for her somewhere amongst the headstones, and she didn't feel much like chatting. She licked her palm and brushed it over her hair, flattening some of the pieces. This was not her morning.

She was working on one remaining clump of hair when something caught her eye. She whipped her head to the left and scanned the field of headstones. Nothing but crumbling marble, overgrown grass, and a few tattered American flags fluttering with the wind. She noticed an old mausoleum in the distance with its light on and squinted to get a better view.

Years ago, someone spent a great deal of money and effort putting little lights by the headstones. Each one pushed into the ground, a light for the dead on the darkest of nights. They were solar lights, though, not running on batteries or electricity. And this morning, the sun was alone in the sky, high and heavy, unaccompanied by a single cloud. Agatha felt its warmth on the back of her neck. How could this grave's light be on?

She stepped off the sidewalk into the cemetery, heading toward the grave, curious about whose name was etched into the stone. The fall leaves crunched like burnt cookies under her shoes, which were not even slightly wet from the rain two days ago. Nothing stayed wet under the Mississippi sun.

She stopped about ten feet before the mausoleum, feeling a pair of eyes on her. She turned to find Leopold behind her.

"Leopold. Geez. Why don't you let me know you're there? Say something."

He smiled, exposing his wayward front tooth. "Sorry. You're going to be late, ya know. Just thought I'd tell you."

He was dressed somewhat normally today, Agatha noticed. A pair of jeans with a short-sleeved black collared shirt and tennis shoes. No bowtie, but she wondered about the collared shirts.

Agatha turned back toward the grave. "I wanted to see why this grave's light was on."

"It's Old Lady Caillavet."

"How'd you know that?"

"Blanche Caillavet? She was some Mardi Gras Queen like a hundred years ago," Leopold explained. "But she used to snatch children and hide their bodies in her shop down in Vieux Marche. Or something like that. At least one kid went missing in her shop. Bobby something. How do you not know Blanche Caillavet? I thought you were from Biloxi, Agatha."

Agatha scowled. "I am from Biloxi, thank you. But no, I've never heard of Blanche Caillavet."

"Maybe you should pay attention in history class, then." Leopold smiled, satisfied with his dig at Agatha. "Seriously, you've never heard that old rhyme?"

"What rhyme?"

"Don't wait until the sun doth set to visit the shop of Blanche Caillavet. A riddle she'll ask to sell you a mask. You and your soul are the debt."

Agatha watched Leopold enjoy himself while reciting the poem. He'd even done his version of a little jig while saying the words. She looked back at the large grey structure with one lone cement angel standing out in front, its head down, hands pressed together in prayer. An iron gate led to the interior of the mausoleum, which housed one marble crypt in the dead center. Agatha could see it from where she stood.

One decaying body inside of that, Agatha thought.

The grave seemed unattended and sad.

"Well, why is her light still on?" she said, changing the subject.

Leopold's smile slipped from his lips. "My grandfather says the lights stay on when the dead have something to tell us."

"Your dead grandfather?" Agatha was the one enjoying herself now.

Leopold's face fell, descending into sadness mixed with a dash of embarrassment. He pulled on the straps of his backpack, tightening them on his shoulders. He turned back toward Irish Hill Drive, walking briskly away from her, unconcerned whether or not she followed him.

His words flew angrily out of his mouth into the wind, which carried them straight back to Agatha with a biting force.

"Better hurry, Agatha. You're going to be late."

CHAPTER 8
AN UNWELCOME SURPRISE

Agatha and Leopold finished the rest of their walk to school in silence—which made Agatha quite content—Leopold used his long, skinny legs as an advantage over Agatha, who trailed behind him several leg lengths.

Second period was nearly halfway through by the time they arrived, and they each received a tardy. Agatha crumpled the small yellow paper between her palms and deposited it in the girls' restroom garbage on her way to Mrs. Wright's English class. She'd intentionally stopped by the bathroom to avoid arriving with Leopold and starting rumors. No need to give any of her classmates any more reason to talk.

She stopped at the classroom door and took a breath. She hated being late. She didn't like the pause and the twenty-five pairs of eyes on her that came with entering a classroom late. Through the small window in the door, she could see Leopold already sitting at his desk. He'd been lucky enough to snag a desk at the back of the room for English. They'd swapped places, really, as her desk was directly front and center of this classroom, which made being late for English even more excruciating.

She took another breath and pulled open the heavy wooden door. As expected, a small silence followed, coupled with several stares. But this morning, Agatha could see most of her classmates were already working on something, their heads down and pencils out.

"Well, good of you to join us this morning, Agatha," Mrs. Wright smiled, a fake smile crossing her face. "Both you and Leopold."

Agatha hated her for that. Her trip to the bathroom had not helped in the slightest.

She kept her head bowed as she found her way to her desk and pulled a black notebook from her backpack.

Mrs. Wright turned her back to Agatha and selected a pink-colored chalk to write on the board. "You nearly missed the big assignment for the quarter. You and Leopold."

Agatha gritted her teeth at the second mention of Leopold. Mrs. Wright was apparently trying to make a point of embarrassing her this morning. She studied her teacher with a scowl, her fat butt cheeks smushed together like two lumpy loaves of bread smothered in a blue cotton dress with yellow flowers on it. In fact, her whole body looked like smashed loaves of bread everywhere, from the back of her arms to the mushy tops of her feet, to the roll on the back of her neck.

Mrs. Wright always wore her black hair pulled back in a severe bun-today was no exception-which emphasized her swollen, pudgy features. Her fleshy face, drowned in too much makeup, always held a permanent, snooty look, which made her unapproachable. Agatha figured she liked it that way.

Her lips formed an upside-down smile, the bottom one jutting out like a bulldog's. And her answer to everything was NO. Can I go to the bathroom? No. Can I ask a question? No. Can I sharpen my pencil? No. Her appearance, coupled with her attitude, was why everyone called her Mrs. Wrong.

Tippy told Agatha she'd heard Mrs. Wright was married, a fact Agatha could hardly believe. Someone married her? She wondered if he liked bread.

"Earth to Mr. Doom. HELLO?" Mrs. Wright was now yelling at Dorian, her large brown cow eyes, decorated in blue eyeshadow, alive with irritation. "You need to put that away and do your work, or else I'm going to take it."

Agatha glanced to her left to see Dorian stuffing the gold coin in his pocket. He looked at her and rolled his eyes. He picked up his pencil, pretending to write feverishly in his notebook, every now and then sending a cutting glare at the teacher.

Mrs. Wright, for all of her heaviness, was quite fast, and Agatha now found her standing in front of her own desk. "Miss Anxious, aren't you going to ask about the assignment you missed because of your tardiness?"

Agatha bit the corner of her left pinky. "Oh. Um, yes, ma'am. What is it?"

"Good of you to ask!" Mrs. Wright narrowed her eyes, pleased with herself. "As you know, Halloween is approaching, and we are doing book reports—don't we all just love book reports—on the legends of the Mississippi Gulf Coast. Now, all your classmates drew a number and actually got to select their topics, one by one. All of them except for you and Mr. Panic, of course. Because you both decided to be late. Together."

Agatha felt her ears redden with exasperation. "I was NOT with Leopold, Mrs. Wright. I woke up late."

Mrs. Wright wiped her round, plump nose with the back of a blubbery hand. "Regardless, you both will have the leftovers. Only two topics left, and I'll draw for you." She shook two folded pieces of paper between her cupped palms, her cheeks jiggling with each exaggerated shake of her hands. She laid one piece of paper on Leopold's desk and waddled back to Agatha's, her butt cheeks in a disagreement beneath the fabric of her dress.

She grasped the remaining piece of paper between two porky fingers, deciding to read it before handing it to Agatha. She snickered and threw the piece of paper on Agatha's desk. "Enjoy," she sneered. "Book reports are due two weeks from today, and try not to Google, folks. I want your behinds IN the libraries checking out books! The reports will be given orally. That means aloud in front of the class for those of you with lesser vocabulary."

Agatha drew in an angry breath, peering over at Dorian, who rolled his eyes again, agreeing with her in their distaste of their English teacher. She looked down at the piece of paper, folded sloppily and slightly crumpled. Indicative of how she imagined every aspect of Mrs. Wright's life to be: sloppy, messy, untidy, hurried.

She snatched the piece of paper up in a huff and unfolded it where she was faced with her teacher's surprisingly perfect cursive handwriting:

Blanche Caillavet – Biloxi's Queen of Mardi Gras.

"OH MY GOD. NO WAY," Leopold said in disbelief as they walked home from school that afternoon. He'd apparently forgiven Agatha for her remark earlier in the day. "The irony. That is W-E- I-R-D. I mean, we were just talking about her."

"I know," Agatha looked down at her shoes as they walked, both her hands on the straps of her backpack. The fact that Leopold now seemed to be her walking home companion hadn't gone unnoticed.

"I mean, cool though, too. I'm a bit jealous. You get the Queen of Mardi Gras who murdered people, and I get some dumb pirate story about Deer Island."

"Well, you can have it. I don't want it." She kicked at a pebble, sending it into the street.

"Highly doubt Mrs. Wrong will let us switch. Not after today, anyway."

"Want to come to my aunt's shop with me?" she suddenly interrupted him. "That's where I go after school every day. She has some interesting stuff, and uh, I don't really feel like being alone, I guess. It's been a weird couple of days."

Leopold tried to conceal his delight. "Um, sure."

They were coming upon the cemetery, and Agatha didn't want to know if the solar light in front of Blanche Caillavet's grave was still on, but she could see in her periphery that it wasn't. Good.

The shop was beautiful and inviting, a quaint little purple house with a purple front porch. A wooden sign, painted white, hung from the roof, welcoming visitors three steps up onto the small porch, beckoning them into the macabre treasures that lived within the walls of Hattie's Odds & Ends.

Leopold stared up at the sign. "I never knew this was your aunt's shop. I've seen this place a thousand times and never been inside, even though I live like right down the street. I think I was too scared to go in, honestly."

"Wuss." Agatha smiled and pushed open the wooden door where a bell announced their arrival.

She looked at her aunt, sitting behind her desk as usual. "That's new." She pointed at the bell.

"Yep. Sure is." Aunt Hattie was toying with one of her two long braids on either side of her shoulders. "Well, who is this, Miz Magnolia?"

Agatha turned to Leopold, who politely introduced himself without any assistance.

"I'm Leopold. Leopold Panic. Nice to meet you, ma'am." He kept his hand on the front door as if ready to escape at any moment.

Aunt Hattie laughed. "No ma'am necessary. You can call me Aunt Hattie. Agatha doesn't bring many friends here, so this is a real treat. Actually, I take that back, she's brought zero friends here, so I'm quite delighted. Are you from around here, Leopold?"

"Yes, ma'am. Er, I mean, yes, Aunt Hattie." He shrugged his shoulders. "I live just a few streets over. On Gill Avenue."

"Ah." Aunt Hattie eyed him for a few seconds too long, producing an awkward moment between the three of them.

"So...." Agatha started, remedying the silence. "The bell? Why?"

Her aunt didn't take her eyes off Leopold. "There is one on the back door, too. Dom kept surprising me. Scared me a couple of times. So, now I know when he's here."

Leopold gave a nervous laugh. "Dumb? Somebody's name is Dumb?"

"No, she said Dom," said Agatha. "You're dumb." "Dom?" said Leopold, suddenly serious.

"Yes. Dom is short for Dominicus," Aunt Hattie answered him, her eyes back to a stack of receipts in front of her. "He's my handyman if you will. He stocks my shelves and unloads boxes for me in the after-noons most days, but you probably won't meet—"

"Yep, that would be me," said a voice down one of the rows. "At your service." Dom appeared at the entrance to Red Rum Row, a broom and dustpan in his hands. He looked toward the three of them, the friendly smile rapidly disappearing from his bearded face.

"Well, alright, then," said Aunt Hattie, confused. "Dom, this is Leop—"

Before she could finish her sentence, the ringing of a bell interrupt-ed her. Agatha turned to see Leopold bolting from the store, the wood-en front door slamming fiercely behind him.

CHAPTER 9
FOLLOW ME HOME

Dom crinkled his forehead as if every last one of his feelings were hurt.

Aunt Hattie didn't move, her eyes studying the front door of the shop. She glanced back toward her stack of receipts. "These can wait. Dom, why don't you head on home? It's nearly closing time anyway."

She turned to her niece. "Want to stay the night with me, Agatha?"

Agatha could sense her aunt was trying to change the subject. "Tonight is a school night," she said, instantly regretting it. She did want to stay the night. The answer to that question was always yes.

"Ah, you're right." Aunt Hattie smiled. "Well, better be on your way home. It looks like that backpack is quite full. You must have homework. Come stay tomorrow night. I mean, that's still a school night, but it's better for me anyway. I have errands to run when you get out of school tomorrow, and you can come with me."

Agatha kept her eyes on the bell above the door. She could still hear the door slamming behind Leopold. So angry. So quick. So full of fear. "Sure." She pushed open the door, and the bell let out a small ding.

"Goodnight, Miz Magnolia."

Agatha didn't have the heart to play their southern nickname game. The door closed behind her, and she stepped off the porch, continuing on Beach Boulevard. Her mother would be home by now, and all she felt like doing was sleeping.

She walked one street past her own to Gill Avenue, trying to determine which house was Leopold's. About ten houses sat on the small street, and Agatha looked for any items she recognized. She didn't know if Leopold owned a bike. Two houses to her right had bikes parked in the carports, but they were both pink. She kept walking, making small mental notes about each home, either checking it in her mind as a possibility or X-ing it off as not being Leopold's.

She passed a lawn with children's toys scattered in every direction. Dirty with mud and mildew, all of them laying in the grass a bit too overgrown. They hadn't been touched in weeks, she gathered. And children? Leopold hadn't mentioned any siblings. *X.*

Two ancient, weathered women chatted at the end of their driveways to Agatha's left, one with a walker and the other keeping her balance on a cane. *Double X*, Agatha thought. The women were far too old to be what Agatha pictured as Leopold's mother. One paused, mid-conversation, to look in Agatha's direction with distaste. Agatha looked away, wondering why old people were so hateful sometimes.

She was approaching the end of Gill Avenue, nearly to Irish Hill Drive. She looked up to see one lone house in the distance on the right and two empty lots to her left. The house was situated at the end of Gill Avenue and had to be Leopold's by process of elimination.

She stood across the street in one of the empty lots, peeking from behind a large oak tree. She squatted beside its trunk, pretending to fumble for something in her backpack but keeping her eyes on the house—a plain, peach-colored house, no bigger than her own. No porch. Just three concrete steps up to a simple brown front door with three small windows at the top. No cars in the carport. It looked as if no one was home, but it was definitely lived in and well kept. The yard was lush and green with perfectly trimmed grass and a few squared-off bushes by the front door.

A small light was on in the front bedroom of the home, the curtains separated in such a way as to allow Agatha to see directly through. Leopold sat at his desk, facing away from the window, his head in his hands. *Check*, she said to herself, satisfied with her investigative skills.

Leopold bent over a book and scribbled on a stack of notebook paper next to it. A couple of times, Agatha saw him lean far back in his chair and sigh, staring straight up to the ceiling, his body limp and lifeless for a few minutes. He was thinking about something that didn't make him happy, Agatha thought.

A fit of coughing broke her concentration, and she looked toward the end of Gill Avenue to see Mr. Dominicus rounding the corner from the beach. He paused, hunched over, his hands on his knees as he finished his coughing. He spit on the ground. Was he following her? Agatha snatched her backpack and disappeared into the high grass of the empty lot toward Azalea Drive and home.

THE FRONT DOOR was locked when she got there, so she knew she'd be alone. She flopped herself face down into her pillow, being careful to glance over at the Scrabble board before doing so. The same twelve letters were still situated in the same twelve spots. She found herself irritated about several different things. Leopold's quick exit. Mrs. Wright being such a jerk. Aunt Hattie taking back her invitation to stay the night. Macbeth needing to be fed. How hot her room was because Taco Chubs was in her parent's bedroom. The stupid letters on the Scrabble board. She wanted to go on. Sometimes whining felt good.

Stupid letters on the Scrabble board. What was she afraid of? Twelve little wooden squares? *Does he want to tell me something? He can pick them up. Or maybe it's a she? Is it a she? What does it want? So, it likes my dog. Does it want my dog? And who is Mary?*

She threw herself onto her bed again. Too many questions. Too many things to think about. Within minutes, she was asleep.

CHAPTER 10
THE LAUNDRY ROOM

Macbeth's husky barking woke her. Sweat pasted Agatha's hair to her face, and some was in her mouth. She wiped it away and glanced toward the window.

It was night, and she was instantly mad with herself. She had so much to do. Research for the book report, math homework, dinner, a bath. And she was starving.

She found her mother at the dining room table, chomping on a bite of fish sticks and macaroni and cheese mixed together—her mother always mixed foods—and a book in her left hand. "Hi, love. Dinner is on the stove." She smiled at her daughter and glanced at her watch, her mouth forming an 'I'm sorry' look. "Oh, God. I'm sorry. I meant to wake you. Yikes. Guess this book is too darn good." She stabbed another wad of macaroni mixture and plopped it in her mouth, returning to her book.

Agatha stood in front of the stove, staring at the fish sticks on her mother's burned cookie pan. She picked one up and nibbled the end. It was cold.

"Do you have any homework?" her mother called from the table.

"Yes," she mumbled, followed by "Don't I always?" under her breath. She dropped the fish stick back on the pan, and it landed with a soggy thud. She headed back to her room.

"I think I'll start it now," she said as she passed her mother. "I'm not hungry anymore." Anita Anxious did not look up from her book.

By the time she reached her room, Agatha had changed her mind, settling on the idea of a bath first. She unbuttoned her dress, one of two dresses she owned with buttons down the front. Her mother knew how to sew on buttons, apparently, but had not figured out pockets. She threw it in her hamper and scanned her hangers for tomorrow's outfit.

One dark green dress hung on a hanger, pushed to the very back of the closet. Agatha's least favorite dress. She couldn't even remember the last time she wore it. The remaining hangers were empty, which meant her clothes hamper was full. She rolled her eyes. Yet another item to add to her list of things to do before bed. Only, this one upset her the most.

She knew her mother would require her to wash her own clothes, and the laundry room was outside the house, in the dark. It gave her the creeps. Not because of the dark, but because of the roaches. She could hear them in there, scurrying every which way with their furry little legs. She shuddered and grabbed her clothes hamper. Maybe her charms would work on her mother tonight.

"Mom," she said as she entered the dining room. "Um, I really need to get started on a book report. Can you put these in the washing machine for me?"

Anita Anxious cocked her head to one side, flashing another 'I'm sorry' look. She was becoming quite good at those, Agatha thought.

"Honey, you know that's your one chore. I'm tired too. But it won't take you two minutes to dump all that in the washer."

Agatha groaned and pulled open the back door. She walked down the two steps from the porch and turned to the splintered, wooden door immediately on her left. It took some effort to open, as usual. The humidity always swelled the door shut, and Agatha had to grasp the knob with two hands. It finally came open, the bottom of the door brushing against the concrete. Agatha saw the top hinge had come loose and wondered if she'd just done that.

Deciding she didn't care if she had, Agatha timidly entered the small room and reached her hand up to where a string hung from the ceiling. She pulled once, and a lone lightbulb clicked on, the laundry room blanketed in a dim, orange light. The walls were concrete and only served to make the small, musty room seem even smaller. A rusty, white washing machine and matching dryer were in front of her. One wooden shelf above them housed the detergent, various unmarked spray bottles and solutions, and a few old clothes pins. Several other shelves were above her to the right and left, where Mr. Anxious kept all of his tools. In the back corner were the mop and broom. The room was a catch-all for tools and cleaning supplies.

Agatha backed out of the laundry room and waited a few moments, listening for any sound of scurrying. She could usually hear the roaches, especially this one roach in particular, who not only seemed to have three generations of family living in the Anxious family laundry room but appeared to have a little bit of weight to him as if he'd been eating quite well his whole life. Agatha called him the Thanksgiving Roach, and she wondered what roaches actually ate as she nibbled her lip.

She waited a minute or two more and heard nothing but silence. Leaving her lip alone, she put one foot in front of the other and stepped back into the laundry room. The lightbulb string dangled above her, and she dumped her clothes in the washing machine along with a couple of dashes of powder. She slammed the lid shut and turned the washer's knob to the quick cycle, reaching for the light string before running from the laundry room. She missed. She stood outside in the grass, debating about the light, ultimately deciding it would be best to leave it on since it would be darker when she returned.

"Atta girl," her mother said as she passed her in the kitchen, donning two yellow gloves. "I would ask you to help with the dishes, but I'll give you a pass tonight. Make sure you get your

bath in, though."

Agatha threw the empty clothes hamper back in her closet and opted for a quick shower instead. The clock in her bedroom read 9:08, and despite her earlier nap, she felt sleepy. She let the warm water from the shower fall over her shoulders like a wet, heavy coat. She lay on the floor of the tub, water pouring over her small body, as she dug her fingers into the nearly used-up bar of Irish Spring. She thought about Leopold, wondering why she was so irritated with him. He hadn't really done anything wrong. Maybe it was his leaving without saying goodbye. Rude at the very least, she decided.

The house seemed extra quiet when she turned off the running water. She saw her terrycloth robe had been laid on the sink. She hadn't heard her mother come in. She dried off and grabbed it, thinking how much she hated the color. Lavender. Her grandmother bought it for her a couple of years ago. It was a sweet present, and Agatha hated to admit she loved how soft the robe felt. But it was lavender. Lavender with yellow stars. Agatha sometimes wondered if anyone in the family besides Aunt Hattie really knew her at all.

"Mom?" she said, swinging open the bathroom door. There was no answer. She stepped into the hallway and winced. She looked down to see one of the Scrabble board pieces stuck in the ball of her foot, its sharp corner piercing a small area of her skin. She plucked it from her foot and turned it over in her palm to find it was a "K." Her fingers toyed with the wooden square as she wondered how the square happened to be in the hallway.

She threw her towel in her hamper and smirked. Her mother would be mad if she knew. Mother always said a towel should be used three times before being put in the dirty clothes. Agatha smiled at her defiance.

With a sigh, she picked up the rest of the Scrabble pieces on her floor. Putting them in a messy pile at the corner of her desk, along with the board itself, she cleared a space for her notebook. She pulled a green binder from her backpack and placed it on the desk, flipping it open to the page where she'd written her book report information earlier in the day. She stared at the words on the page.

Blanche Caillavet - Biloxi's Queen of Mardi Gras.

She slammed the notebook closed. Going back to the laundry room suddenly seemed more appealing than doing research on creepy

Blanche Caillavet, whoever she was. The hair on her arms stood up just thinking about the rhyme Leopold had recited. She tore a piece of paper from her notepad on her desk and scribbled a few words outside of the lines. She folded it twice before writing "Leopold" on the outside and placing it in a side pocket of her backpack.

Her mother's door was closed, she noticed, as she headed toward the laundry room, a small bit of light shining from the crack near the floor. She must be reading.

Agatha swallowed hard as she stepped off the back porch and stood in front of the laundry room. The door was shut again, and from the crack near the hinge, she could tell the light inside was off, both facts which Agatha knew with certainty were incorrect. I never would've shut the door, she thought, remembering how difficult it had been to open.

She heard scuttling behind the door and stayed frozen where she was, listening to the sounds around her as the darkness of the evening settled in. The wooden clothes pins hung loosely on the old wires of the clothesline. The creaking chains on her old swing set, which she was much too mature to use. The car noises-horns and engines-from Beach Boulevard just off in the distance. And yet, the loudest sound to her at that moment was the scuttling behind the laundry room door.

She thought about going to get her mother but knew she'd tell Agatha there was 'nothing to be afraid of.' Agatha was learning there was quite a lot in the world to be afraid of.

She thought about calling Aunt Hattie, but what could she do from so far away? And even so, what would Agatha say?

"Aunt Hattie, can you come get my laundry out of the washer and put it in the dryer for me?" Sure. That sounded great. Thirteen years old and afraid of a few roaches.

This last thought irritated her. She gritted her teeth and placed her hand on the knob of the door, yanking it open as hard as she could. She expected to see the Thanksgiving Roach and four of his siblings nibbling on something or scurrying away. Instead, Agatha was met with the color white. The box of detergent was upside down on the floor of the room, its powdery contents everywhere as if someone had deliberately pushed it from the wooden shelf.

The powder itself was undisturbed, a smooth canvas of white coating the concrete floor. No roaches anywhere. The only sound she heard now was the cars in the distance, and even the wind seemed to have stopped.

Agatha groaned and reached for the broom and dustpan, careful not to step into the pile of detergent. As she did, the scuttling sound returned, and something ran across her foot. She screamed, backing out of the laundry room and dropping the broom. She scanned the small room, looking for any sign of the Thanksgiving Roach.

And then she saw it. She'd been wrong.

There, in the darkest corner of the room, lit by its own chalky color, was a hand. A skeleton's hand from the wrist down, propped up on all five fingers and poised to move. Agatha could see sand and seaweed caught in the joints between the bones. A salty, fish-smelling water dripped down to the tips of the fingers, the foul scent invading Agatha's nostrils from where she stood. The pointer and middle fingers scraped themselves against the ground, bone meeting concrete in a hard, seemingly desperate motion. Over and over as if deciding something.

Thirteen-year-old Agatha Anxious watched in horror, her mouth stretched open in a perfect circle, as the hand, complete with the grace and quickness of an eight-legged arachnid, crawled across the floor to the pile of undisturbed detergent, hastily scrawling its urgent message to her:

Give it back.

CHAPTER 11
VIEUX MARCHE

The next day, Agatha could barely concentrate. The whole morning had been a blur. She trudged like a zombie, limp and lifeless, from class to class. In her head, she

kept hearing the scratching noise of the hand against the concrete, its fingers moving the detergent aside to leave its message for her. What followed kept playing in her mind on repeat: her running up the back porch stairs and falling, scraping her knee, running to her bedroom, and slamming the door, which surprisingly didn't wake her mother, hiding under the bedcovers with all the lights on until the early morning hours.

She hadn't slept a wink. Instead of curling up on the couch, Macbeth slept beside her, under the covers, too, while she jumped at every noise she heard during the witching hours of the night.

She hadn't finished her laundry, either. She couldn't. She wasn't even sure she could go back to the laundry room to fetch her clothes ever again. She was apparently doomed to wear the dark green dress forever, she thought, as she'd yanked it on that morning. Green. What a gross color.

She knew her mother would discover the wet clothes still waiting in the washer sometime today, not to mention a laundry room floor covered in detergent, and Agatha fully expected a reprimand when she got home. But tonight, she was staying with Aunt Hattie, a small relief since she could avoid the punishment for one more day.

Agatha ran the whole mile from the school to Aunt Hattie's shop, a mix of emotions in her belly. Excitement. Fear. Dread. Wonder. She arrived to find her aunt waiting for her on the front porch of the shop.

"You ready, Miz Magnolia?" Aunt Hattie's hair was back in the two devilish buns she'd worn a few days before. She'd paired a black tank top with a colorful, multi-ruffled skirt to her ankles. Aunt Hattie never showed her legs. Agatha wasn't sure she'd ever seen them. But she imagined they were just as tan and thin as the rest of her body. "I closed up early. Lots to do!"

"Where to first?"

"Vieux Marche first. Then the grocery store. I'm out of popcorn. Can you believe it? Me? Out of popcorn on a night my favorite niece is staying? Unforgivable. Absolutely unforgivable."

Agatha laughed. She was Aunt Hattie's only niece. But being her aunt's favorite was still pretty special.

They hopped into Aunt Hattie's truck and headed down Beach Boulevard with the windows rolled down, Agatha taking in the salty air, but this time something was different. The stinky, fishy smell she usually loved held a familiarity that wasn't quite so pleasant. The skeleton hand from the night before flashed in her mind, the brown water dripping down its knuckles onto the laundry room floor. It smelled like beach water. Biloxi Beach water.

She rolled the window up.

"It'll get hot in here, Miz Magnolia. Roll that back down, sugar. You know my air conditioner don't work."

Agatha did as her aunt instructed, but she tried to breathe through her mouth to avoid smelling the air.

They turned into Vieux Marche, one small road with various quaint shops on either side. At its beginning, Vieux Marche was a segment of Pass Christian-Point Cadet Road and was later named Howard Avenue.

It was the heart of downtown Biloxi and, in the early part of the century, housed banks, department stores, and theaters on either side of the street.

Renamed Vieux Marche in the 1970s—French for 'Old Market'—it presently housed just a few various shops of interest frequented by locals. Agatha noted how old some of the shops were as they pulled into a parking spot, a few with signs boasting their beginnings in the 1890s.

"Alrighty, love," Aunt Hattie said, turning off the ignition. "I'm going over there." She pointed to a drugstore wedged between an art supply store and a small furniture store. "You coming?"

Agatha looked down at her hands in her lap and shrugged her shoulders.

"Want me to meet you at the fountain?" Aunt Hattie snickered, and Agatha shot her a look.

The fountain housed a large statue that Agatha loathed. A fifteen-foot-tall man bent forward, his arms ominously outstretched in mid-throw of a cast net. He was surrounded by a circular pool of water and was made of bronze-colored metal. His bald head, bland features, and hooked nose gave him a frightening appearance, along with two black holes in the metal where his eyes were supposed to be. He was called The Golden Fisherman, and Agatha considered him to be the thing nightmares were made of. She'd had dreams of him stepping off his pedestal in the fountain and prowling the long street of Vieux Marche after dark, looking for humans to collect in his cast net. She hated him.

"Absolutely not," Agatha said, looking around. The words had barely left her lips before she saw Dorian entering a small shop with a purple awning two doors down from the fountain. "I'll be right back, Aunt Hattie."

Aunt Hattie grabbed Agatha by the arm. "I'd appreciate you staying outside and talking to your friend. Don't go inside anywhere."

"Why?"

Aunt Hattie released her grip and smiled. "It will just be hard to find you. I mean, look at all these shops. How will I know which one you went in?"

"But—" Agatha started.

"And because I said so." Aunt Hattie was already outside the truck, but her eyes held Agatha's gaze. "Isn't that what parents always say? Meet me back here in ten minutes."

Agatha walked the short distance until she stood under the purple awning. Professionally-painted gold letters outlined in black adorned the front window of the shop: Doom's Maskerades, it read. And then, underneath: "est. 1987."

The door swung open, and out stepped Dorian, a broom and dustpan in his hand. "Hi, Agatha," he said, his deep voice making Agatha's heart skip a beat.

"Hi," she said sheepishly, holding her hands behind her back so she could pick at a few of the dry cuticles.

A moment passed where neither said anything, Dorian finally breaking the silence. "You gonna come in?"

"Oh, uh, no. I'm just waiting on my aunt," Agatha said, motioning toward the drugstore. "So, this place sells masks?" Oh, my God. Did you just ask that, Agatha? Really? Its sign says MASK SHOP. Agatha clenched her teeth.

Dorian arched his mouth into a sly smile, exposing a few perfectly straight teeth, and Agatha felt her heart do another flip flop. "Yes. Yes, we do."

"We?"

"Yes. My family... I work here. After school...I mean. My family owns it...forever. I mean, a long time." Dorian

fumbling over his words amused Agatha. He pointed to the front window. "Since 1987."

"I see," she said, kicking at a couple of pebbles on the sidewalk. "You work here every day?"

"Just school days. After school." "For how long? Hours?"

"No. Just until five o'clock, when we close," he said, pointing back toward the black lettering on the store's front window where the shop's hours were clearly posted. "I wouldn't stay here after dark anyway," he added, his tone quieter.

Agatha stopped kicking at the pebbles and looked up. "Why's that?"

Dorian cleared his throat and swallowed hard. "Because," he said. "Things happen here after dark."

Agatha didn't know what to say, and she didn't want to know what he meant. "So, where is your coin?" she said, steering the conversation in a different direction altogether.

Dorian seemed disappointed with this new topic of talk. "I lost it."

"You lost it?" "Yes."

"It was probably worth a million dollars, and you lost it?" she laughed.

Dorian cleared his throat. "Well, I didn't really lose it. It's here." He motioned back toward the shop behind him. "I've just misplaced it inside the shop."

"Oh, so you just can't find it."

"Yes."

Agatha tugged at the neck of her green dress, where her mother had sewn a small lace collar. She scratched at it. She hated collars, and it was another reason she hated the green dress. "I always try to think of the last place I remember having an item. Usually, I can find it if I do that," she told Dorian.

He kicked at the same two pebbles and lowered his voice to a mumble. "Yeah, well, the last place I had it was near the back of the shop."

"Ok."

"I was sort of throwing it in the air, and I dropped it." He kicked one pebble out into the street. "And it rolled into the back room. There's a curtain back there, and it rolled under the curtain into that back room."

"Ok?"

Dorian picked up the last pebble and threw it as far as he could down the street. "I don't go back there. As I said, things happen here after dark. Especially in-"

"Agatha, are you ready?" Aunt Hattie called from in front of the drugstore. Agatha motioned for her aunt to come to her. She wanted to introduce her to Dorian, mainly so she could talk to her aunt about him later. Aunt Hattie shook her head and stayed put.

"Aunt Hattie, come meet my friend," Agatha said, running to her and grabbing her hand.

Aunt Hattie wriggled out of Agatha's grip. "No. He can come to me."

Agatha detected defiance in her aunt's voice. "Is something wrong, Auntie?"

Aunt Hattie kept her eyes on Dorian, who put his hand up in a friendly wave that wasn't returned. Aunt Hattie steered Agatha by the shoulders to the passenger side of the truck. She hurried Agatha into her seat and slammed the door. "I don't want you anywhere near that shop, Agatha. Bad things happen there after dark."

CHAPTER 12
UNLESS YOU HAVE TO

"What in the world was that all about?" Agatha said as her aunt sped out of Vieux Marche, keeping her head bowed in embarrassment. In front of Dorian Doom of all people. She watched him from the passenger side mirror, shrugging his shoulders as he went back inside the mask shop.

Her aunt was silent for a few moments. "I already told you, Agatha. It's just that shop. I don't want you near it. Now, let's change the subject, shall we? I want to hear about your ghost."

The memory of the skeleton hand made her queasy. "Where are we going now?" Agatha whined.

"The Biloxi Library," her aunt answered pointedly. "Now, your ghost."

"What about him?"

"Is it a *him*?"

Agatha bit a piece of loose skin from one of her knuckles. Precisely the question she'd been wondering the night before. "I really don't know. I think so. I feel that way, but I don't know how I know that."

Aunt Hattie held her pointer finger in the air, making a statement. "Always go with your gut, Agatha. Your gut and your intuition will never steer you wrong. Someday, your life may depend on it."

Agatha was not enjoying her aunt's sudden serious, matter-of-fact mood. "Ok, then, I guess it's a HE."

Her aunt sat back in her driver's seat and took a breath. Her shoulders relaxed. "Ok, what else? What did the skull jar say?"

Agatha surveyed her other knuckles to see if there was any skin needing removal. Suddenly she felt like talking. "The jar said, Mary."

"Mary?"

"Yes, Mary. I don't know what it means. And then the second time he contacted me, he wrote on my Scrabble board."

Aunt Hattie guffawed, enjoying herself. "Genius!" Aunt Hattie patted Agatha on the leg. "Sorry, it's just always amusing how creative some ghosts can be. Please, go on."

Agatha folded her arms. "The Scrabble board said, 'I like your dog.' Like, all one word across the board. Macbeth had been growling at something in the corner where my desk was. And then he wrote on the board, 'I like your dog.'"

"Ah, so he's just being friendly there," Aunt Hattie nodded her head. "That isn't a clue. He was just being nice, I'm guessing."

"I guess." Agatha wasn't sure. "Either way, and then, last night..." she stopped mid-sentence, envisioning the skeleton hand in the detergent.

"Yes?"

"Then last night, another message. But this time, in the laundry room—"

Aunt Hattie made a gagging noise. "Ugh, I hate that laundry room. Not sure why your dad hasn't fixed it up. I mean at least a new coat of paint or somethin'. Doesn't make any darn sense to me. Just creepy and oh, those darn roaches..." She looked over at

her niece, who was silent. "Sorry. Sorry. Continue."

"This time, Aunt Hattie, he purposely spilled detergent all over the floor and wrote me a message."

"Oh, wow." Aunt Hattie was suddenly intrigued.

"But not just that, I actually saw a...a hand. A skeleton hand." "A skeleton hand?"

"Yes, a hand. Of bone. It crawled across the floor like a gross little spider and wrote its message in the detergent."

Aunt Hattie stared straight ahead, unblinking. "He's creative. Got to give him that." Then, after a minute or two of thought, "I think he might be materializing."

"What does that mean?"

"Meaning, he will show you more of himself every time he contacts you."

Agatha crinkled her face. "Eww. I hope not. I don't want to see any more." Her mouth filled with saliva, and she forced it down her throat.

"Oh, ginger muffins! I've got to get in the left lane," Aunt Hattie said aloud, turning on her blinker. "So, what did the message say?"

"It said 'give it back.'"

Aunt Hattie snapped her fingers. "Ah! See. There it is. Ok, it wants something back."

Agatha rolled her eyes. "Really, Auntie? Of course, he wants something back. I *did* figure that much out."

"Crap-a-dap!" Aunt Hattie suddenly groaned. "I missed my turn. Guess I'll have to keep going on to Lee Street. Gosh, I hate Lee Street." Agatha could tell she was talking to herself now, distracted and seemingly unaware Agatha was still in the car. Some days, Aunt Hattie could rattle on for three or four minutes to herself, and Agatha found it entertaining to watch. Today was not one of those days.

"You know what," Aunt Hattie said, suddenly determined. "Since we're turning on Howard Avenue, I guess I better show you something before we go to the library." She took a left onto Howard from Lee Street and, after a few blocks, slowed the truck to a crawl as they passed several businesses and an empty parking lot on their right.

Aunt Hattie pulled next to the curb and put her truck in park. She pointed across the street. Agatha followed her aunt's thin finger with her eyes toward a red brick business with windows and four fancy white columns surrounding the entrance. Agatha read the sign, even though she was already familiar with the place. "Benford-O'Malley?"

Aunt Hattie nodded her head in agreement. "Yes."

Agatha waited for her aunt to say something more, and when she didn't, she filled the empty air between them with words. "What about it? Pop Pop's funeral was here a long time ago," she said, referring to her grandfather.

"Someone lives there."

This time it was Agatha who chortled. "Auntie, nobody lives there."

Aunt Hattie grabbed her niece's hand. "Listen to me."

Agatha's smile dropped from her face. She didn't like whatever had gotten into Aunt Hattie this afternoon.

"Someone does live there," her aunt continued. "In the funeral home? How? Who? The owner?"

"Listen, Agatha!" Aunt Hattie grabbed her chin, pulling Agatha's face close to hers. "He was the undertaker, but he lives there. Or, rather, he's never left. Read the sign again."

Agatha squinted to read the smaller lettering under "Benford-O'Malley Funeral Home, Inc." She made out the cursive font after a few seconds. *Since 1899.* And then beneath that, *Lucius Nikolai, Founder, and Undertaker.*

"Ok?" she said, turning back to her aunt. Then, the thought dawned on her, the realization spreading over her like a warm blanket, starting at her neck and shoulders, the warmth working its way down to her calves and ankles. She wiggled her toes to shake off the thought. "Is...is Lucius Nikolai still alive or something?"

"Well, kind of." Aunt Hattie smiled.

"How? He'd be over a hundred and fifty years or something," Agatha hated math and wasn't going to even try to do it in her head.

"Eh-eh-eh," her aunt shook her finger in her face. "We don't ask that. *All* things are possible, right? There is no "how" or "why" when you're a Perceiver, Agatha."

Agatha kept quiet.

Aunt Hattie continued. "According to the obituaries, Mr. Nikolai died decades ago. And he did, but he most definitely is still there and only visible to Perceivers and those who are 'sensitive' to seeing ghosts. Mr. Nikolai, he's...he's....he knows things. He's neither good nor bad, and he helps. Sometimes. He's a very tricky character, I guess, and he can be dangerous; you must know that."

"I...I don't understand, Auntie." She didn't.

"I know you don't. And I'm doing a terrible job explaining it." Her aunt let go of her chin, putting both of her hands in her lap. She played with a ruffle of her skirt. "Mr. Nikolai is sort of an all-knowing being. He keeps the balance between...let's just say, good and evil. The living and the dead. He can help Perceivers, but it comes at a cost. He always asks for something from you, so be prepared to give," Aunt Hattie paused, looking out her window, reliving a memory. "I've only gone to see him once, Agatha. And I pray you never have to. But I felt obligated to tell you about him. Never. Never go there unless you're in desperate need or it's absolutely necessary..." Aunt Hattie's voice broke as she trailed off. Agatha thought her aunt might cry.

Aunt Hattie grabbed a tissue from the glove compartment and blew her nose. "And that's all I want to say about that. Ok?" She turned to Agatha, two watery eyes full of tears that refused to fall. "Unless you have to, Agatha. Unless you have to."

Agatha hesitated. "Why would I ever need to go there?"

Aunt Hattie blew her nose into the napkin again and wadded it up, tightening her hand around the ball of tissue until her knuckles were white. "I hate to give examples, Agatha. I believe that sometimes if words are spoken aloud, they might happen just because you've said those words." She grabbed another tissue from the glove compartment. "Maybe you'll have a ghost that's angry or being difficult. Something like that is why you might go to see him. A situation you can't solve on your own. That's all I want to say. Really." She threw the wadded napkins into the cupholder between the seats.

"Auntie?"

"Yes, love?"

"Was there ever a ghost you couldn't help?"

Her aunt closed her eyes and inhaled a breath heavy with concern. "Yes, love."

"Who?"

"A woman."

"Where?"

Aunt Hattie threw the truck in gear and pressed down on the pedal as she did a U-turn toward the library. "At that mask shop in Vieux Marche."

CHAPTER 13
THE SWITCH

They pulled into a parking spot at the Biloxi Public Library. Agatha had a thousand questions, none of which she asked. She could tell her aunt wanted no

more talk of prior ghosts, so she didn't press her. Instead, she grabbed her backpack from the truck. Perhaps she could get some work done on the book report while they were at the library.

"What are we here for, Aunt Hattie?" said Agatha, taking a chewed pencil with no eraser from her backpack and sticking it behind her ear as she climbed the library's grey cement steps.

Her aunt, now recovered from their previous conversation, pressed both hands to the buns atop her head, squeezing them to check for any loose strands. "I have a few books to pick up, love. It might be a little while. Is that alright? Then we'll head on over to the grocery store for popcorn."

Agatha scanned the open room of the library's first floor and found Leopold sitting at a table by himself near the back windows. "I have a book report to work on anyway." She headed in Leopold's direction. "Not to mention a few questions I need answers to," she said to herself.

Leopold sat with his back to the windows, a pencil sideways in his mouth while he flipped through the pages of a tattered hardback. He would abruptly stop on a page when he thought he saw something he needed. Then, with a sigh, he kept flipping. Agatha watched him do this a few times from a distance before approaching.

"Good afternoon, Mr. Panic."

Leopold looked up, and the pencil fell from his lips, missing the table altogether and landing in his lap.

Agatha cut him off before he could say anything. "How'd you get here?"

He grabbed the pencil from his lap without taking his eyes off Agatha. "I rode my bike."

"You have a bike?"

"Don't most people have a bike? Is that weird to you?"

Agatha threw her backpack in the chair opposite Leopold and sat next to him without being invited. "You know, I could ask you why you decided to leave my aunt's shop yesterday. So rude, by the way. I mean, rude with a capital R. And I've been pretty annoyed about it. But I decided I needed a favor from you, so I'm not really mad anymore. I was going to give this to you tomorrow, but—"

She reached into a side pocket of her bag and grabbed the note she'd folded the night before. She tossed it in front of him, where it landed face up. He could read his name in her handwriting. Printed. All caps. No frills or curls or bubbly letters. Besides her dresses, Agatha was very un-girly.

She smiled. "So, we're even."

Leopold looked at Agatha and back at the piece of paper twice before opening it and reading it aloud. "Can we switch?"

"Yeah, that's what it says." "Switch what?"

"Book reports."

Leopold crumbled her note, squeezing it tight in the palm of his hand. "For Mrs. Wrong? No way. I've already written like three pages on my topic."

"You owe me."

Leopold was indignant. "How so? Because I left your aunt's shop yesterday? Come on."

"Yes!" Agatha answered a bit too shrilly. She cleared her throat and lowered her voice. "Yes, but really, I can't do mine. I just can't."

Now Leopold smiled. "Why? Scared of 'ole Blanche Caillavet?" He threw his head back and snickered to himself.

"No. Or yes. Maybe. I have no idea, but I do know I'm NOT doing that book report because she creeps me out. Please, Leopold?"

Leopold stared for a few seconds at Agatha, gauging her sincerity. When he'd decided she was being genuine, he let out a sigh. "Fine."

He grabbed a notebook from under the tattered hardback he'd been reading earlier and pulled a piece of paper from one of its pockets. Before handing it to her, he said, "I'm guessing you want the pages I already wrote, too?"

Agatha bit the inside of her cheek. "Maybe just so I can read through? I won't copy anything. I promise."

Leopold grabbed three more pieces of paper from the same notebook and handed them to Agatha. "Don't have any use for them anymore anyway. Just don't copy them word for word. I don't want to get in trouble with Mrs. Wright."

He packed his notebook and pencil back in his bag but left the tattered book on the library table. He pushed it toward Agatha. "You'll need this. It's where I got most of my information." Then, with a look of sarcasm crossing his face as if mocking Agatha for a bad trade of book reports, he added, "Hope you like women pirates."

CHAPTER 14
WHAT IT WANTS

Agatha sat in the car while Aunt Hattie went into the grocery store, reemerging minutes later with a bag of popcorn kernels, a six-pack of L&C Root Beer, two bags

of black licorice, and a smile as wide as Mrs. Wright's hips, Agatha thought. Aunt Hattie knew her niece was not the typical Biloxian. She preferred L&C Root Beer to the locally-made Ruff's brand. It was something they'd playfully debated for years.

"But Ruff's is tuff! " Agatha could hear Aunt Hattie saying in her head, poking fun at the company's slogan.

"Well, it's crappy stuff!" had always been Agatha's quick reply before the two would erupt in cackles.

"Thanks, Aunt Hattie," Agatha said as her aunt climbed into the driver's side and started the engine.

"Of course! Now, we just have to decide on which movie to rent. Whatcha thinking?" she asked Agatha as she tore open one of the bags and placed a long whip of licorice in her mouth.

Agatha grabbed one too. "Something scary." "Tell me something I don't know, love."

Agatha gave a little laugh as they drove to Aunt Hattie's house in the middle of nowhere, Agatha trying to suppress her need to bring up the mask shop and the funeral home again.

"Was that the boy who left my shop yesterday?" Aunt Hattie finally said when they pulled into her driveway.

Agatha wondered why her aunt wanted to know. "Yes."

"Mmm," she said absently as she grabbed the bags of groceries. She hoisted a foot to the driver's side door and kicked it closed. On her way into the house, she cooed and talked childishly to the cats who followed her to the doorstep. "Yes, ma'am, Miss Maggie-Moo and ya'll too, Greta-Boo-Boo and Bert. I'll have your meals out in a few minutes. Just a second, my little sweets."

Agatha planted herself at the small dining room table while her aunt heated the cats' milk. She pulled Leopold's four sheets of paper from her backpack, where she'd loosely stuffed them as she left the library. For the first time, she took a good look at the book report topic he'd written down while in Mrs. Wright's class:

Mark Read – The Deer Island Pirate.

Agatha read it a couple of times over. "I thought he said it was a woman pirate?" she said aloud.

"Hmm?" Aunt Hattie was behind her, stirring the bowls of milk, pausing to taste it to make sure it wasn't too hot for the cats.

"Nothing. Just that book report I've got to work on for English."

"What's it about?"

"Just legends and lore around this area. We had to draw our topics. Well, I mean, I didn't get to. And then I ended up switching with Leopold because I didn't like mine, and—"

Aunt Hattie was suddenly interested. "Nice. Lots of legends and lore around here. What's your topic?"

Agatha looked again at the paper. "Mark Read, The Deer Island Pirate? Sounds boring."

Aunt Hattie balanced three bowls of milk in her hands. "I know that one. It's very interesting. Sweets, can you get the door for me?"

Agatha held the door for her aunt while she fed her cats, sweetly singing to them while they lapped their warm milk. Agatha planted herself again at the kitchen table, chewing the end of the pencil missing its eraser, wondering about Leopold and who his parents were, why he left Aunt Hattie's shop the previous day, and how he managed to always have such a dramatic exit after a pretty awesome one-liner.

"So, Mark Read, eh?"

Agatha had been so wrapped up in her thoughts she hadn't noticed her aunt sitting next to her at the table. "Yes. The Deer Island Pirate."

Aunt Hattie tucked a piece of Agatha's shaggy blonde hair behind her ear. "What are you so deep in thought about, Agatha? What movie do you want to watch this evening?"

Agatha looked down at her gnawed pencil. Saliva covered its wooden middle, and she wiped it on her dress before tucking it behind her ear. "Nothing, really. Leopold said this topic was about women pirates. I was just confused."

"Well, that's because Mark Read was actually a woman," her aunt said. "She was a woman pirate who paraded around like a man because, well, women pirates weren't exactly popular back then."

"Really?"

"Yep," Aunt Hattie said, retrieving the bowls of milk from the porch and rinsing them out in the sink. "Dressed like a man most of her life, I believe. Even fought in a battle. I'm sure you'll read all that in the book there," she said, motioning toward the book Leopold had given Agatha, half of it protruding from her backpack on the table.

Agatha grabbed it and turned a few pages. The writing was small, and she felt her head throb, her pulse now in her forehead. The book was huge in her small hands, and Leopold hadn't marked or saved any of the pages. "Well, what was her real name, then?"

Aunt Hattie cocked her head upward as if she might find the answer on the ceiling. "Hmm," she said, putting her hand to her chin and rubbing it a few times. "I actually don't know. Well, I do know, but I can't remember." She squinted as if squeezing her eyelids together would summon the name. "I'll think of it here shortly," she said, relaxing. "You going to work on that report, or are we going to watch a movie?"

Agatha rubbed the space between her eyes and slammed the book closed. Its binding made a long, drawn-out creak as if the book was deciding whether or not to fall apart. "I'm going to get my pajamas on, Auntie. I'll be right back."

"I'll make some popcorn!" Aunt Hattie called as Agatha grabbed her backpack and made her way down the small, narrow hallway to the last door on the left.

Her aunt loved dark colors, Agatha thought as she poked her head into the dark bedroom with smoky grey walls that served as Aunt Hattie's bedroom. It was sparsely decorated, with a twin bed in one corner and a small grey nightstand beside it. A crooked tower of old books and magazines sat atop the nightstand, and another of Aunt Hattie's colorful pair of reading glasses balanced themselves on top of the very highest book. Agatha scanned the walls, each with a unique mirror on it. Large, medium, small, ornate, framed, gold, silver. Once, Agatha had counted fifty-seven mirrors. Agatha never questioned the mirror collection. Aunt Hattie was known to collect quite a few strange items.

Among the various mirrors were a few framed black and white family portraits, the subjects caught in various poses. Some smiling, some serious. Agatha ran her fingers along a few of the frames, trying to name each person. She knew her grandfather and grandmother, even though they'd died when she was four and six, respectively. Three photos of Aunt Hattie as a child. In one photograph of her grandfather unwrapping a Christmas present, joy spread over his face.

Agatha smiled when she came to a black and white photo of her father, Sonny, as a teenager. His gym shorts were a little too short, and his curly black hair was a little too long, just touching his shoulders. His tight white tank top bore the letters "BHS" for Biloxi High School, and in his right hand, he held a pole used for pole vaulting. Agatha giggled. Her father still held the state record in pole vaulting, a fact she dared not share with any of her friends. That wasn't the sort of thing you could brag about.

She was turning to leave when one photograph caught her eye. This one had the privilege of being on top of Aunt Hattie's nightstand. Agatha found it poking from underneath the stack of books. A simple photograph of a blonde teenage boy staring into the camera, his eyes wide with what Agatha perceived to be sadness. A few mountains stood in the distance behind him, and the muted colors of the photograph told her it was old.

This boy was probably an old person now, and she wondered where he was and if he was still sad. She gently pulled the photo out from under the books to get a closer look. She faced a boy who seemed not only sad but troubled. Heavy with the burdens of the world or the future that lay before him. She wondered what bothered him and why Aunt Hattie would keep such a sad picture. She turned the photograph over to see a small note scribbled in faded blue ink. Take care, Hattie. I'll see you soon—love, your brother Timmy.

A lump formed in the back of Agatha's throat, and she set the picture back where she'd found it, exiting Aunt Hattie's room as quickly as she could. She tiptoed down the hall toward her purple bedroom, relieved her aunt was still making popcorn in the kitchen. She passed a dark navy bathroom to her right but decided she didn't have to pee.

She pushed open the door to find the room exactly as it always was, dark and lovely with an antique feel. The four-poster bed had a red bedspread on it, its edges neatly tucked under the mattress. Agatha was careful to place her backpack next to the bed and not on the comforter. Two old, beaded lamps sat atop two nightstands on either side of the queen-sized bed. Their gold and white beads dangling in neat rows reminded Agatha of a shaggy dog she'd once seen on television called a Puli.

She yanked the cord on the nearest lamp, and a yellow glow lit the room, the soft light falling on a massive, dark brown wardrobe occupying the farthest corner. It stood there in a creepy sort of way, Agatha thought. This brooding piece of furniture with its groaning drawers and two heavy doors seemed out of place. If furniture were alive and had feelings, Agatha was sure the wardrobe would be wearing a permanent frown.

Perhaps it was the fact that Aunt Hattie kept a lot of her own mother's clothes in the wardrobe. Agatha's grandmother had been dead for seven years. The knowledge that her dead grandmother's dresses and aprons were hanging from the wire hangers inside the wardrobe gave Agatha the creeps.

Sometimes, on the nights she stayed at Aunt Hattie's, she was sure she could hear those hangers creaking, their rusty, curved tops dragging against the metal rod from which they hung, a slow, scraping left and right. It was as if her grandmother's ghost was fingering each of her clothes, searching for something to wear from beyond.

Agatha shook off the thought and opened one of the nightstand drawers where her aunt kept a pair of her pajamas. She and Aunt Hattie's overnight escapades were rarely planned and having some clothes at her aunt's made it incredibly convenient.

As she slid her arms into a solid black nightdress with twelve black buttons down the front, she marveled at how soft the fabric was. Smooth and lightweight against her skin. It was so comfy, and she didn't mind the girly ruffles at the ends of the sleeves.

"Auntie, is the popcorn ready?" she yelled as she finished the last of the buttons on the nightgown and threw the green dress with the lace collar on the floor, refusing to hang it up. Its ugliness didn't deserve a hanger.

There was no answer, but she thought she heard a muffled pop-pop-pop sound from down the hall. Aunt Hattie made it the good old-fashioned way. Kernels in oil in a pan on the stove. Microwave popcorn was beneath Aunt Hattie, and Agatha agreed. Nothing tasted as good as stove-popped popcorn with butter and salt.

"Aunt Hattie!" Agatha yelled from deeper in her belly as she turned to the door. She saw it was closed, and a chill tickled her spine. She never shut bedroom doors. Never.

A squeak exited her lips, but it was all she could manage. She considered inching her way toward the door but thought better of it. What if someone or something was waiting behind it?

A scratching noise caught her attention. Softly at first, then harder. Longer. More drawn out. She looked around frantically, immediately resting her eyes on the wardrobe. Anything bad or scary had to be coming from the wardrobe, right? But the sound was closer to the floor. Hesitant, she moved her eyes downward. A bubble of saliva lingered on her lips as she realized the noise was from under the bed.

She wanted to be strong, brave enough to lift the lace bed skirt and see what was underneath, but she could not muster the strength. Unsteady on her feet, she backed up toward the closet. Once she felt the door behind her, she slid down the wall until her butt rested on the floor. Fear encompassed her, and she jammed a thumb into her mouth, tearing away at the side skin until she tasted blood in her mouth.

The scratching noise continued in a motion toward her until Agatha saw the bed skirt move. And then a finger, followed by a thumb and four more fingers until it was a whole hand jutting out from beneath the bed. Agatha saw it was using its bluish nails to dig into the floor in an effort to propel itself forward, which it did a few more times until it revealed an entire arm—no bigger than Agatha's own—whitish and wet, blue veins protruding beneath the cold skin.

I think he might be materializing.

She heard Aunt Hattie's voice from earlier in the day. Was that just this afternoon? Seemed like days ago now. Her aunt was right. He had progressed.

Agatha wiped her thumb on her nightdress, careful to keep her eyes on the arm sticking out from under the bed. For a few moments, it lay motionless. Agatha held her breath, wondering if the arm knew she was there. *Of course, it does.*

Slowly, the hand and arm turned itself upside down, palm upwards, its four fingers beckoning for Agatha to come closer. She stayed put and shook her head furiously as if the hand could see her adamantly telling it no.

Suddenly, it righted itself—palm down—and, placing its index finger and thumb finger together, the hand began to write something on the floor, an imaginary pencil pinched between the two fingers. It continued this motion, over and over, writing one single word and then starting at the beginning again, repeating itself.

Agatha moved her fingers to her head to find the gnawed pencil she'd placed there earlier, still wedged between her skull and her ear, waiting for use. She grabbed it and threw it at the hand. Immediately seizing the pencil, the hand then rewrote the single word on the floor for Agatha to read, the same childish scribble she'd seen on the note from the jar:

treasure

Agatha took a few moments to read the word, trying to understand what the hand asked of her. Suddenly, the hand pushed the pencil back in her direction, which wobbled toward her, rolling in a lopsided direction from all the dents and bitemarks, coming to rest near her knee. She grasped the pencil, feeling its wetness between her fingers, understanding this to be an invitation.

An invitation to ask a question. An invitation to communicate. On the floor next to her, in all capital letters, she neatly wrote: WHERE

She pushed the pencil back toward the waiting arm and hand. As she did so, a thought popped into her head. A memory from a few days ago. Was this what the hand wanted? A feeling of dread started at her toes and worked its way up toward her stomach, where it manifested into a weighted ball of nausea.

The hand once again took the pencil, its fingers slipping and squishing around the wood as it wrote another single word, this time in all capital letters, mimicking Agatha's handwriting. It left spaces between the letters in the word until a familiar face flashed in Agatha's mind:

D O R I A N

When it finished the last letter in the name, it threw the pencil at Agatha angrily and with more force and strength than she expected the hand to have. She leaped from her spot against the closet, lunging toward the bedroom door's knob, twisting it in one swift motion, throwing herself into the hallway, where she hit her head against the wall. She sprinted down the hallway toward the living room, her socks slipping on the wooden floor.

"Sweets! I got it. It just came to me." Aunt Hattie was facing away from her, banging a small, old television remote against the palm of her hand. "Well, crumbly nibbles!" she muttered to herself as the back of the remote popped open, and two batteries

flew out. "It was Mary."

Agatha stood, one foot in the living room, one in the hallway, un-blinking until the dryness of her eyes produced two tears that dripped down her cheek. She tasted the saltiness as one reached the corner of her mouth. "Wh-what, auntie?" she murmured in a daze.

"Your book report. The name. Mark Read. You know, the Deer Is-land Pirate who was a woman?" her aunt said, on her hands and knees, searching for the batteries. "Her real name was Mary."

CHAPTER 15
POPCORN AND PIRATES

Agatha had only a small recollection of the next few moments. She recalled Aunt Hattie picking her up off the floor and laying her on the couch.She must have fainted. After coming to, the words sprang from her lips in a feverish rush. She made no effort to stop them.

"It wants the coin, Auntie! The coin! He told me he wanted the coin. He actually talked to me this time. I asked him a question, and he answered. His arm. His whole arm..." she trailed off as her aunt wiped her face with a cool rag.

"Shhhh," Aunt Hattie whispered to her. "Speak slower. What happened? You scared the squiggles out of me, Agatha!"

Agatha took a breath and held it, counting to five. She released the air at the same time she released the words. "The ghost. He talked to me again. Just now. In the back room." She paused to swallow. "This time, I saw his whole arm. It was small and blue with blue veins. And the same fishy smell I smelled when I saw the skeleton hand." Agatha buried her face in the washcloth, finding comfort in its coolness.

"What did he say to you, Agatha?" Her aunt pushed her hair, damp with sweat, off of her face.

"He scribbled on a piece of paper. And it said, 'treasure.' So, I decided to see if it would answer me. If I could ask it a question. And he let me."

"Go on," her aunt pressed her.

"I wrote on the piece of paper, 'where?' Because I didn't know what he was talking about. I truly had no idea, Auntie! And then he wrote again. 'Dorian.'" Agatha sat back against the couch, silent. Aunt Hattie looked confused as if waiting for more of the story.

"I know what he wants, Aunt Hattie." "What?"

"My friend at that mask shop today, the one who wanted to meet you."

"Yes?"

"His name is Dorian."

"Why would the ghost want Dorian?"

"No, no, Auntie." Agatha shook her head. "Dorian found a gold coin on Deer Island last weekend. We had to give short presentations about our weekend in Mr. Barone's class. That's how I know. He showed it to all of us. He found it right on the beach, and I think the ghost wants that coin back."

Aunt Hattie sat back against the couch next to Agatha, both of them facing forward, wide-eyed. Her mouth was open for a long moment. Finally, she spoke. "It's a doubloon."

Agatha didn't move. "A what?" Both were speaking in the same direction and not at each other.

"It's a larger coin, isn't it?" "Yes, Auntie."

"Poorly made?"

"Yes."

"Could be an old Spanish coin called an Escudo." "Escudo," Agatha repeated.

"Sometimes I call them doubloons," her aunt explained. "But in the golden age of piracy—that is, when pirates controlled the high seas—the coins were called Escudos. I think. I'm pretty sure. A little history lesson for you there," Aunt Hattie nudged Agatha with her elbow.

"Ok?"

"Well, if what you've told me, as far as your clues go, sounds like you've got the Deer Island Ghost, sugar." Aunt Hattie grinned from ear to ear, her thin cheekbones pushing further upwards until they were nearly under her eyes. "Didn't you say the message inside the jar said, 'Mary?'"

Agatha nodded.

"And the second message was 'give it back,' or something like that."

Agatha nodded again.

"Ok, well, now he's telling you he wants the treasure that apparently your friend Dorian has, which he stole from Deer Island, right?"

Agatha finally spoke. "Yes. Well, I mean, 'stole' is a strong word, but I guess that's what he did. I don't know."

Aunt Hattie slapped her knee. "Well, there it is! Mystery solved. You've got to get that coin and bring it back to Deer Island. Then your ghost will be happy, and you'll have finished your first Perceiver mission."

Agatha closed her eyes, thinking for a moment. "I'm sorry. What do Mary and Mark Read and pirates have to do with this ghost, though? Is this the ghost of Mary?"

"Let me get the popcorn for that," Aunt Hattie said, eagerly springing from the couch for the kitchen, returning within seconds with a large bowl of buttered popcorn. She placed it in Agatha's lap.

"A long time ago, there were pirates in these waters, Agatha. Right here off Biloxi—oh, you better take mental notes because if this is what your book report is on, I'm pretty much giving you all the information you'll need." she popped a few kernels of popcorn in her mouth and continued, chewing with her mouth open. "So anyway, people don't really know who the pirate was, but it was rumored to be either Jean Lafitte or Mark Read, who was also known as Mary. I think we've established that Mark Read was really a woman whose name was Mary, right?" She looked at Agatha, awaiting a reply.

"Uh-huh," was all that came from Agatha's mouth.

"Ok, so good 'ol Pirate Mary landed on Deer Island, it's rumored—I like to say that because there's really no evidence, but it's always been rumored—that she parked her butt on Deer Island to bury a treasure.

People have searched for it for centuries and never found a thing. But either way, she came ashore and asked some of her crew—again, allegedly she did this—who would like to 'guard the treasure.'" Aunt Hattie put her fingers in the air and made quotes with her fingers as she said the last part.

Agatha looked down at the bowl of popcorn. Her aunt had prepared it beautifully, but she wasn't hungry. Her aunt's hand came crashing into the bowl, grabbing a handful of kernels, which she absentmindedly threw into her mouth as she kept talking.

"So, this novice deckhand or cabin boy, who had no idea what he was doing, raised his hand. Volunteered. Ya know, to guard the treasure. And just like that, she lopped his head right off."

Agatha finally looked up from the popcorn. "What?"

"Yep. And then buried his body with the treasure. See, what she meant by 'guard the treasure' was 'guard the treasure for eternity' if you get what I'm saying." She winked at Agatha, crunching down on another handful of popcorn. "So, that ghost is supposed to guard the treasure. Like, forever. That's his job. And I suspect that your friend Dorian happened to find one of those coins and took it home, and now the ghost wants it back so he can continue doing his duty."

Aunt Hattie let out a breath, exhausted. "How incredible. You get the Deer Island Ghost! Folks have been talking about that treasure around here for a hundred years. Was the arm small?"

"The arm?"

"Yeah, that blue arm you saw just now. The one that wrote the last message." Aunt Hattie was clearly unbothered about the possibility of a severed ghost arm having been in one of her bedrooms.

"Yes, actually. It was," Agatha said, crinkling her forehead.

Aunt Hattie shook her head. "Yup. It was always rumored that the deckhand who volunteered was a young boy. Probably your age, come to think of it. A headless skeleton boy. Again, rumored."

Agatha put the bowl of popcorn in her aunt's lap and placed her head in her hands.

"Oh, come on, sweets. What's wrong? This is easy," Aunt Hattie said, giving her a squeeze around the shoulders. "You've just got to get that coin from Dorian and make a trip to Deer Island and bury it some-where. That's probably it. I can't go with you, but I'm sure you can find somebody with a jet ski or a small canoe or something and row out there. It's not far." She loaded another handful into her mouth. "This is so good. I can't stop."

"It's not that easy, Auntie." "Why?"

"Because when I talked to Dorian today, he said he lost it." "Huh? How could he lose it? That thing is probably worth a

pretty penny!"

"I know. Well," Agatha said, correcting herself. "It's not really lost, he said. It's just misplaced, I guess."

"Where'd he last have it?" Her aunt asked. "I always start with the last—"

"Yes, I know," Agatha interrupted her. "That's what I told him. To start where he last had it."

"Well, where did he last have it?"

Agatha finally turned to face her aunt, locking eyes with her. She wanted to see her reaction as she spoke the words, to understand her aunt's true feelings about what Agatha now knew she had to do. And the things she might encounter while doing them.

"Auntie, the coin is in the back room of Doom's Maskerades."

CHAPTER 16
FACE TO FACE

The next thing Agatha knew, popcorn was everywhere, Aunt Hattie having launched it from her lap as she flew off the couch. Her aunt crunched several kernels under

her feet as she headed to the kitchen, frantically looking for something.

"Where is your backpack, Agatha?" Aunt Hattie's voice was two octaves higher than usual.

"In the bedroom. On the floor next to the bed. Why?"

There was no response. Aunt Hattie was halfway down the hall before Agatha could blink and returned with the backpack before she could blink again. She stuffed Agatha's green dress into one of its front pockets. "Let's go."

Agatha didn't understand. "What? Where? I thought we were watching a mov-"

"I'm taking you home," Aunt Hattie cut her off. "Whyyyy??" Agatha whined.

"Because. Um, you fell. And you probably hurt yourself. And you probably should be home. You know, with your parents. If you hurt yourself, that is. Just to be safe." She threw a forced smile Agatha's way.

"Auntie, I'm fine. I was just scared for a moment. That's all."

Aunt Hattie grabbed her by the arm, leading her out of the house, down the front steps, and past the white cats whose evening naps were suddenly interrupted. They scrambled away- one hissing her displeasure-and Aunt Hattie threw open the passenger door for Agatha and tossed her backpack onto the floorboard.

"Aunt Hattie, I'm fine!" Agatha said louder. Maybe her aunt hadn't heard her the first time.

Aunt Hattie said nothing in return. In fact, she was silent the entire twenty-five-minute drive to Agatha's house. She faced forward, concentrating and fingering her spiral necklace, her thumb and index finger finding its grooves. At times, she seemed to be squeezing it or enclosing her palm around it while mouthing a few silent words, although Agatha could not determine what she was saying.

They pulled into the small driveway, Aunt Hattie sweating and Agatha disappointed at how the night had turned out. *Stupid Deer Island Ghost,* she thought to herself. *What did I say to upset Aunt Hattie?*

"Agatha."

"Yes?"

"Listen, love. I'll call you tomorrow. You can stay then, ok? I really just want to make sure you are ok and figured you would be safest at home with your mom and dad."

Safest? Agatha caught the word mid-air and toyed with it in her mind for a few seconds, wondering what her aunt meant by that. "Ok," she said, finally.

She grabbed her backpack with a sigh and gave her aunt a melancholy look, hoping her sad brown eyes would somehow make her aunt feel bad.

It didn't work. Aunt Hattie was determined.

"Love you," Agatha said as she opened the door and stepped out, the grass wet beneath her bare feet. She'd forgotten she was still wearing the nightdress. She'd have to remember to return it tomorrow.

"And I love you, Miz Magnolia," Aunt Hattie replied, a smile crossing her mouth but worry in her eyes. "Oh, Agatha?"

"Yes, Auntie?"

"Before we left, I heard you say you were scared."

"Yes. I guess about the ghost."

"You've got to stop being scared. That ghost needs your help. We all need a little help sometimes, don't we?"

"I guess so," Agatha said, not sure what her aunt was getting at.

"Goodnight, love. And remember, you've got a gift. It's a powerful thing to be a Perceiver."

Agatha closed the door and stood on the front porch, watching her aunt throw the truck into reverse and back out of the yard. She could hear it sputtering all the way down Azalea and watched as the two tail-lights took a left onto Beach Boulevard and disappeared from view.

Why is she taking a left? Her house is to the right. Agatha nibbled the side of her thumb for a few moments, bewildered, before turning the knob and going inside.

AUNT HATTIE PULLED into Vieux Marche and silently slid her truck into a parking spot near the Golden Fisherman, her right hand still clasped around her spiral necklace. She exited her vehicle and scowled as she stared into the blank, lifeless face of the statue. "Agatha has good reason to hate you," she said to it.

She wiped her brow as she planted herself under the familiar purple awning of Doom's Maskerades, its gold lettering catching the light of the moon, popping off of the glass, and shouting at Hattie as she stared them down. She let go of her necklace and fished in her pocket, producing a single silver skeleton key, shiny and untarnished by years of use. She quietly placed the key into the shop's front door keyhole and turned it slowly as if concerned about waking something on the other side of the door. She heard a click, and the door opened a crack.

"Haven't changed the locks in all these years, I see," she whispered to herself. "Tsk. Tsk." She pocketed the key and tiptoed inside, closing the door softly behind her.

One long aisle stretched out before her, specialty masks in glass cases on either side. Both walls to her left and right were floor-to-ceiling mirrors, giving the impression the tiny shop was larger than it really was, and hundreds of masks were attached to them of differing colors, sizes, faces, moods, and emotions. Some of the pairs scowled down at her with devilish smiles as if they knew she was where she didn't belong. She inched forward, catching her reflection in one of the mirrors. The wooden floorboards underneath her feet groaned. Some in low notes. Some, an octave higher.

Straight ahead, at the back of the shop, a black velvet curtain hung from the ceiling, its heavy fabric stopping about an inch from the floor. *If it touched the floor, Dorian's coin would've never rolled back there, and we wouldn't have this problem. And I absolutely wouldn't be here,* Hattie said to herself.

She took the time to examine each specialty mask in the cases on either side of her, some made of porcelain and some of paper mâché. Pairs of jesters, male and female. One pair, the king and queen of all different suits of cards. Another was a blue velvet with bells on the ends of the fabric around the porcelain faces, and a final pair was decorated with sheets of music fanned out and outlined in gold paint.

Hattie continued down the lone aisle toward the black curtain which separated the mask shop into two rooms: the sales floor and the backroom workshop. She paused to glare at a single mask in the corner, on display in its own glass case. If she hadn't been less than fond of its former owner, the item most likely would've been something seen upon the shelves of Red Rum Row at Hattie's Odds & Ends.

It was on full display, positioned on a silver stand inside the glass box. A porcelain mask shaped like a cat's head, silver with thin, black intricate lines. Swirls. Circles. Diamonds. A crisscross pattern. Glitter on the ears and nose and beautiful in its complexity. Four wire whiskers protruded from the cat's cheeks on both sides, and there were holes where the eyes would've been. The cat's forehead and eyebrows cast a wicked scowl, and its painted black lips modeled a permanent smirk. A red ribbon was tied to the mask for a prospective wearer to fasten to their head. Beneath the glass box was an engraved bronze nameplate, the font immaculate and fancy:

Blanche N. Caillavet – Mardi Gras Queen, 1937

Hattie shuddered and faced back toward the black curtain, drawing in a long breath. She again clutched her spiral necklace in her left hand, her trembling right one clasping the curtain and gently pulling it aside. Hattie waited for her eyes to adjust, but she could see nothing. She propped open one side of the black curtain and entered the room. In the dark, she could make out the outline of a long table in the center of the workroom, bits of masks strewn here and there. Baubles. Beads. Crystals. Ribbon. Three pairs of scissors. Various cutting tools and craft knives. Hundreds of jars of paints and paintbrushes of various sizes in containers against the wall.

Unfinished masks hung on the wall in front of her, four of them missing half their faces. A silver cat mask with black lips, identical to the one in the glass case, hung in the corner. Two masks looked broken, cracked in several areas, and glued back together. *Perhaps the owner was trying to salvage them for selling at a lower price,* Hattie thought to herself. *Who would buy those?* She snickered, a nervous little giggle that echoed off the four walls of the workroom.

She was still talking to herself and shaking her head at the thought of Dorian's father when she noticed the silver cat mask with black lips was no longer in the corner but to her left.

It had moved.

Hattie took three steps backward, keeping her eyes on the mask as it got brighter and brighter. Balls of light pulsed behind the mask in a hypnotic rhythm as it floated airily toward her.

"Harriet Marigold Anxious," a voice behind the mask said, husky and deep, though still a woman's. "So, we meet again."

Aunt Hattie stumbled backward into the curtain, pulling it from the ceiling and entangling herself as it fell around her.

The mask continued toward her, airily and light but with a purpose. "My, my, how you've aged," said the voice again.

Aunt Hattie fell to her knees, weakened, as the mask approached her further, stopping a few inches from her face. "But then again, so have I."

A wrinkled, grey hand removed the cat mask, and Aunt Hattie looked into the face she hadn't seen in decades. One she hoped she'd never see again. A face that had encompassed her nightmares, thoughts, and dreams for nearly forty years.

The face blinded her. Weakened her. Held her.

Hattie's mouth hung open as tendrils of light extended from the face toward her until they carefully encountered her. They caressed the contours of her face like fingers, outlining her nose, her cheekbones, her lips. They coiled themselves around her ears and threaded themselves through her hair until her two buns fell in waves around her frozen face. They stroked her chin and spiraled themselves gently around her throat.

And then, satisfied with what they'd inspected, the tendrils momentarily withdrew, before extending again in a swift, forceful motion, directly into Hattie's open mouth. She made one long choking noise as she grasped her long, skinny fingers around her own neck. Her mouth opened and closed in rapid movements, in desperate need of oxygen and air. She fell to her side, her head hitting the cold wooden floor. The wrinkled hand placed the cat mask onto Aunt Hattie's face, grasped her ankle, and pulled her limp body into the back room.

And Doom's Maskerades was silent.

CHAPTER 17
ABANDONED

The sun rose the next morning—a Friday—as if nothing in the universe had changed, and Agatha awoke with a headache. She rubbed her left temple and found it was

tender, a small, foggy token of the evening before. The hallway, the hand, the message. The want of a treasure. Dorian's treasure.

She rolled over and groaned. Macbeth was seated at the foot of the bed, eyes closed, his black fur gently rising and falling with his sleepy breaths. Agatha went to her closet to find it full of her dresses. She breathed a sigh of relief that was short-lived. She knew a reprimand awaited her after school.

She threw on a grey dress with thin black vertical stripes. One of her only dresses with a pattern in its fabric. She grabbed a pair of black stockings and her shoes before slipping out into the hallway. She peered into her parents' bedroom. Her father was fast asleep, on his back, his arms crisscrossed behind his head. He must have come home late. Her mother's side of the bed was empty, and Agatha knew she would find her in the kitchen making breakfast.

She was right.

Anita Anxious stood over the stove, wrapping her hair in a bun over a skillet full of eggs and chunks of ham. Two pieces of toast eagerly popped out of the toaster, awaiting their bath of butter and jelly.

"Hungry?" her mother said, not looking in her direction.

Not really, Agatha thought to herself but knew she generally felt better with a full stomach before the start of a school day. "Sure," she said, climbing into a chair in front of Porkchop Cupcake, who wasn't turned on, and Agatha wondered why. The house was stuffy. The stagnant air hung heavily, a stifling blanket of humidity.

Her mother laid a plate in front of her. "Next time, finish your own laundry, please." She squeezed Agatha's shoulders, and Agatha was thankful she'd escaped a punishment.

Upon further inspection of her plate, Agatha saw the ham and eggs were mushed between two pieces of jellied toast to form one awkward sandwich. She peeled back the toast and picked at the eggs until most of them were gone. Then, gulping down her orange juice, she grabbed her backpack, threw her mother a kiss, and left the house. She'd awoken earlier than usual and decided to swing by Aunt Hattie's shop before school.

When she arrived, the CLOSED sign still hung crookedly from the front door. Agatha checked her watch, an old digital one her father had given her a few years ago. She liked it because it was masculine. Probably a boy's watch, but Agatha preferred it that way.

It read 7:45 a.m. Aunt Hattie's shop opened at nine, but it was out of the ordinary for Aunt Hattie not to be at work. She generally spent over an hour at the shop balancing her receipts and doing some ordering and tidying before opening her doors. Agatha frowned but gave it no further thought. She was about to be late for school.

TWO POP QUIZZES, one test, one break, and one lunch period later, Agatha found herself about to leave Art class when she was stopped by Tippy Trinkle, the dark-haired girl from Mr. Barone's class.

"Hey," Tippy said. She watched Agatha pack her backpack and walked with her to the lockers. Agatha's locker happened to be beneath Tippy's. "Want to stay the night?"

Agatha looked at her in shock. Agatha didn't know Tippy considered her a friend, or at the very least, an acquaintance worth having a sleepover with. Agatha didn't know Tippy but judging from her name-brand clothes and shoes, her perfectly styled hair, and her immaculate makeup, she imagined Tippy was pretty wealthy. She also knew Tippy had one of those old antebellum homes on the beach. Why would she want to hang out with someone like Agatha Anxious from Azalea Street?

"I have plans with my aunt tonight," Agatha blurted out without really thinking, instantly regretting it. There was something about Tippy that interested Agatha, and the invite intrigued her more.

"Ok," Tippy said, closing her front teeth around a piece of grape gum. "Just, dunno." She shrugged. "You seem cool. Thought I'd offer." Tippy's long black hair hung to her waist, and she flicked it over her shoulder.

Cool? No one had ever called Agatha that before. Squirrelly?

Sure. Weird? Odd? Yep. But cool? No, never.

Agatha kind of liked it.

Tippy slammed her locker shut. "Plus, Bunny can't."

Ah, there it was. Tippy's best friend Bunny was unavailable, so Agatha was the second choice. *Or third or beyond, maybe*, she thought. Who knows where she was situated in the line of sleepover candidates for Tippy Trinkle in her big house on Biloxi Beach?

"Here's my number if you change your mind." Tippy tore a piece of notebook paper from her binder and wrote the seven digits in large bubbly letters with a purple pen. "See ya." She flicked her hair again and was gone.

A couple of hours later, Agatha was standing in exactly the same spot she'd stood that morning: on the purple porch of Aunt Hattie's Odds & Ends, facing the same crooked CLOSED sign. What was going on? Aunt Hattie never closed her store except for major holidays. She'd never been sick in all the years Agatha had been alive. And even in the event of an emergency, she surely would've left word for Agatha because she knew Agatha would stop by after school.

Agatha nervously bit some dry skin on the fingerprint pad of her thumb, deciding what to do. Finally, figuring she did not have much choice, she cut through the cemetery, pausing at her uncle's grave to pick away a few pieces of wayward grass, cleaning up around the edges of the tombstone to distract her from her worries. After a few more minutes of mindless cleanup, she trudged home.

Dinner with both her parents present at the table was a rare treat for Agatha, but she couldn't enjoy it. She picked at her mashed potatoes and chicken nuggets, pressing down onto the soggy asparagus until it squished beneath her fork. It was canned, she knew. She'd heard fresh asparagus was far tastier and firmer, but she'd never tried it. The Anxious family rarely bought fresh vegetables because they were too much money. Besides, canned vegetables were just as good, her mother said.

Noticing his daughter's absence in the conversation, her father turned to her. "How about you, Agatha? Why so glum? Bad week at school?"

She looked up to find her dad's warm face smiling back at her. It reminded her of her aunt's. Those same, cozy doe eyes beset in a tanned face, his black hair in frizzy waves atop his head. His eyes held a small amount of concern. Agatha knew she could always count on her father to care.

"My week was fine. But it's Aunt Hattie."

"Yes, I know she dropped you off earlier than you wanted last night," her father replied. "Try not to take it too personally, Agatha."

"It's not that, Dad. It's that her shop was closed this afternoon when I stopped by after school. She never closes her shop."

Sonny Anxious' eyes widened a bit, and he looked at his wife. "That is strange. I've never known Harriet to close her shop. I mean, if something came up, she would've told us." He continued to talk to his wife as if Agatha were no longer at the table. "Wonder if it's still closed now. Let me call over there."

He stood in the doorway between the kitchen and dining room, dialing his sister's telephone number, his face contorting into a deeper expression of concern with every unanswered ring. He hung up and began dialing again. "Let me try again. Maybe I dialed the number wrong."

Still, the call went unanswered.

Anita Anxious began to clear the table, somewhat unbothered by the present situation. "Honey, it's nearly six o'clock. Is her shop even still open at this time?" She set the dishes in the sink and ran water over them, scrubbing away while awaiting an answer.

"She closes at seven," Agatha finally said. Always an odd number, she thought. "Opens at nine and closes at seven."

Her father grabbed his hat and headed toward the front door. "Well, one easy way to solve this. I'm going to run over there real quick."

"And what if it's still closed, Sonny?" her mother asked him, her soapy hands propped on the edge of the sink.

He fumbled through the numerous keys on the ring, finding the right one for the family car. "Well, then I'll have to run by her house, honey." He threw open the front door and leaned back inside to reassure his daughter. "Don't worry, Agatha. I'm sure she's at home, and we are worrying for nothing. I'll be back in a jiffy."

He winked at her and was gone.

AGATHA WAS IN HER PAJAMAS, pretending to sleep, when she heard the front door open three hours later. Worry filled her head to foot, but she dared not move. If she didn't go see what her father had to say, maybe it would change things. Maybe everything would be alright if she didn't know the truth. If she ignored what her gut was telling her.

She heard him toss his keys into the bowl by the front door and pull out a chair at the dining room table. Muffled words followed, both her parents' voices carrying through the living room and down the small hallway to where Agatha lay motionless on her bed. A few of the words were whispered, and she thought she heard one small gasp from her mother.

Unable to bear it any longer, she ripped off her covers and stomped to the living room, making sure her footfalls were heard on the wooden floor, announcing her arrival to her parents.

"What is going on?" she shouted in their direction, her voice full of desperation. "Just tell me!"

Her father rubbed his temples, his eyes closed. He patted the seat next to him, beckoning Agatha to sit down. She did so without being asked twice.

"Agatha," he said as he took her small hand in his. "Her shop was still closed, and no one was at her home. You know this isn't like Aunt Hattie. She wouldn't go anywhere without telling us. She's a creature of routine."

Agatha nodded, looking at her father's hand on hers. The velvety smoothness of his palm comforted her.

He cleared his throat. "So, I decided to drive around Biloxi to see if I could find anything before going to the police. I went to all her usual spots, the grocery store to see if she'd gotten groceries, the library, a couple of gas stations, and even back by her store to make sure she hadn't stopped by there. I even drove through the cemetery to make sure she wasn't at...the grave." Agatha noticed his avoidance of her uncle's name. "Nothing. Nothing at all."

Agatha sat back. No news was at least good news. Perhaps she was somewhere else for the night they weren't aware of, and she'd be back tomorrow, her happy, lively self at her store, her hair in a ponytail or two braids or two buns, smiling from behind her desk. Agatha's lips curled into a small smile, completely swallowed in the brief moment of hope.

Her father squeezed her hand to get her attention. "Agatha," he said.

"Hmm?" she turned to face him. She looked over at her mother, noticing for the first time her flushed cheeks and watery eyes.

"I found nothing until..." her father paused to swallow and lick his lips. "...until I drove through Vieux Marche. That's where I found it."

"It?" Agatha managed to say through a couple of shortened breaths.

Her father shook his head. "Yes. Her truck. Abandoned. Right in front of the Golden Fisherman."

CHAPTER 18
A LIE AND AN ADVENTURE

*A*unt Hattie is missing.

Agatha replayed those words repeatedly in her head as she lay on her bed, her clock reading 3:27 in the morning. There was no way she could sleep. This was all her fault. She knew exactly what happened to Aunt Hattie, not that she could tell her parents. Not at the table while they teared up about her aunt. Not while they called the police and went down to the station to speak with someone. Agatha knew the truth and could say nothing.

Her aunt had gone to Doom's Maskerades to save Agatha the trouble. Or the danger. She'd put herself in harm's way so that Agatha would not have to, and in an effort to get Dorian's coin, something happened to her there. She went into the shop and did not come out. Agatha closed her eyes with the thought. She felt tears well up behind her eyelids.

"Bad things happen here at night."

She wanted to call Dorian and ask him exactly what that meant but knew he would think she was a lunatic. She thought of all the people she knew, their faces running in a slideshow through her brain. Who could help her? Who would understand? Surely not any of her teachers. Not her parents. Not Dorian or Tippy. Leopold? Maybe. He did say he saw his dead grandfather from time to time.

Her thoughts fluttered back to Tippy. Tippy surely would not understand, but perhaps she could be of some assistance.

The next morning, Agatha made herself presentable bright and early, combing her kinked bob down with some water in an effort to tame it. She poured herself a bowl of cereal and waited for her father to get up. He would be the more lenient of her two parents, and she hoped to catch him first.

As expected, her father stumbled toward the coffee maker around thirty minutes later, right past his daughter at the dining room table. After pouring himself a cup, he slid into a chair next to her. "Morning, Agatha. Couldn't sleep?"

She shook her head no, waiting a few more seconds before changing the subject. "So...there's this girl at school. Tippy. Tippy Trinkle?"

Mr. Anxious nodded as he sipped his coffee.

"Well, she invited me to stay the night. I mean, she did last night. And I said no because I was so worried about Aunt Hattie. But I called her this morning and asked if I could stay tonight instead. Just to...get my mind off of things? And she said yes."

Her father thought for a few moments, adding a few more sugar cubes to his mug. "Sure," he said. "Why not? We could all use a little distraction. Just make sure I have her phone number. Let me know when to drop you off."

"Uh, actually, she lives right over on Gill Avenue," Agatha lied. "So, I can walk."

"Even better," her father smiled. "You'll be close if any news about Harriet comes up. Just don't forget to leave the number."

"Thanks, Dad," Agatha said. "I'll probably walk over around six or so?"

Her father crinkled his face. "Mmm, make it around 5:30. I want you over there before it gets dark."

"Ok," she called back to him as she skipped off to her room. Once there, she grabbed a small bag, jamming it full of any and every item she thought would be 'essential.' A flashlight. A dark hat and sweatshirt if she needed a disguise or if the place was cold. Black licorice if she got hungry. A pencil and notepad if she needed to take notes in case she forgot something important. Her cell phone in case things went awry. Her toothbrush and hairbrush, and small travel-size body wash made it look like she intended to stay the night at Tippy's.

She peeked back into the dining room and saw her father wasn't at the table. She heard the shower running and, assuming he was in there, dialed Tippy's number on her phone. Thankfully, Tippy answered, and not one of her parents.

"Tippy," Agatha whispered. "It's Agatha." "Yeah? What's up?"

"Your offer from yesterday?"

"What offer?" Tippy said, smacking what sounded like a large wad of gum between her lips. "And why are you talking so low? I can't hear you."

Agatha raised her voice a bit, looking down the hallway to see if either of her parents were coming out of the bedroom. "Your offer to stay the night."

"What about it?" Tippy blew a bubble and popped it directly into the receiver.

"I need to stay tonight. Er, I mean, I need to pretend to stay tonight."

Tippy blew another bubble, waiting a few agonizing moments for Agatha to wonder what was going through her mind. "Ahh," she said, finally. "You're telling your parents a fib? Where ya goin'?"

Agatha ignored her. "Can you cover for me? Please? Like, in case my parents call? I mean, they won't. They never do, plus I have my own cell phone now but just in case?"

"What's in it for me?" It sounded like Tippy was playing with her gum, and Agatha had a vision of her pulling it from her mouth in one long rope, winding it around and around her finger while she toyed with Agatha on the phone.

"More gum?" It was the only thing Agatha could think of at the moment. She realized she didn't know Tippy very well. Her likes. Her dislikes. Her favorite things. Nothing.

"I want you to do my math homework next week," was Tippy's requirement. "No matter how many assignments Mr. Thomas gives us. I hate math. Oh, and more gum is nice. I love gum."

"Yes. Yes. Whatever you want," Agatha heard the shower curtain being drawn open and lowered her voice back to a whisper. "I've got to go. My parents think I'm coming over around five thirty, ok? Just in case they call."

"Sure," Tippy popped another bubble.

"Repeat back to me what I just said," Agatha told her. "You're pretending to come over at five-thirty and lie to your parents if they call."

"No homework help if you don't, Tippy," Agatha attempted to sound stern.

"I got it," Tippy said. "Hey, how'd you know I liked gum?"

Agatha acted like she hadn't heard the question and hung up.

AGATHA SPENT most of that Saturday pretending to do homework in her room so her parents wouldn't bother her. When five o'clock rolled around, she tore a sheet of paper from one of her notebooks and wrote a letter to her parents. In the event she didn't return, she wanted them to know where she'd gone and that she loved them. She folded it as small as she could and stuffed it under her pillow on her bed.

Her mother was starting dinner as she went to kiss her goodbye. She handed her a note with Tippy's phone number on it. "I'll be back for breakfast," she said. "We're just going to play some board games and stuff. She wanted help with this book report we have to do for English, too. And maybe some math homework. You know, Tippy isn't the best student." She realized she'd volunteered all of that information without being asked, and it sounded very much like a fat bundle of lies. Shut up.

"Alright, sweetie. Have fun. She's just a street over?"

"Yes, ma'am. On Gill Avenue. I'll text you when I get there."

"Ok, have a fun time." Anita Anxious kissed her daughter's cheek.

Agatha raced out the front door and over to Leopold's house, sitting in the vacant lot across the street to text her parents, crossing her fingers they wouldn't call Tippy at any point during the evening. If they did, her whole mission pretty much hinged on Tippy remembering to lie for her.

She waited there until it got dark, then climbed the steps in front of Leopold's house and knocked, unsure what she would say if his parents answered. Thankfully, Leopold came to the door. His face bore no expression of surprise or shock at having Agatha Anxious on his front porch on a Saturday evening. "Hi," he smiled. "Are we going on an adventure?"

Relieved he required no explanation, and she said, "Do you have a bike?"

"I have two. Be right back." He shut the door in her face, and she heard the lock click into place. He soon appeared in his carport. He wheeled a rusty orange bike over to her and went back to retrieve a blue one.

"Um, your parents...do you need to tell them—"

"No," he cut her off. "They're not home anyway, and I'm thankful to be getting out of here. My grandfather's been lumbering around the house for the last few hours. He's usually gone in the afternoons, but I can hear him." His dark green eyes burned into hers, and she knew exactly what he meant.

"Follow me," she said, turning her bike toward Irish Hill Drive.

They took a few back roads, Agatha careful to avoid the Biloxi Police Department and Beach Boulevard in case her parents had gone out for a last-minute emergency errand. Not only was she not where she was supposed to be, but she was also out and about. After dark. With a boy. She couldn't fathom the amount of trouble or explaining she'd have to do if someone saw her riding her bike at that moment.

Twenty minutes later, they crossed over Main Street and stopped in front of a business on Howard Avenue, parking their bikes in exactly the same location Agatha had sat with her aunt just a couple days before. Agatha led them behind the brick building, laying her bike on its side under a nearby bush, her backpack tucked neatly beside it. She faced a few of the back windows, deciding if any looked unlocked or open.

Leopold was still on his bike, his eyes fixated on the red brick structure looming before him like an approaching storm. "This?" he asked her, his voice cracking with the one-syllable word. "This is your adventure?"

"Yes," Agatha steeled herself, clenching her fists, then planting her hands firmly on either side of one of the windows. "Benford- O'Malley Funeral Home."

CHAPTER 19
MR. LUCIUS NIKOLAI, UNDERTAKER

Agatha left Leopold, who refused to accompany her, waiting by the bush behind the funeral home. She'd found the window unlocked and wondered if this were

her lucky night or if Mr. Nikolai had known she was coming. She guessed the latter. Crawling through the window had been quick, her small body passing easily through the space, even though it only opened a third of the way. She wiped off her dress, inspecting her stockings for tears, of which she found none.

She leaned her head back out of the window. "Hand me my flashlight."

Leopold followed orders.

"If I am not out in ten minutes, knock three times on the front door. Hard."

Leopold checked his watch and gave her a thumbs-up, running back to where the bikes lay.

"Or bust it down if you have to," she started to worry. She liked having an escape plan for everything and wasn't quite sure what this current situation would require.

Leopold nodded, tucking his hair incessantly behind his ear, uncertainty in his eyes, and Agatha wondered if Leopold would ever be knocking down any doors for her.

She left the window open and faced the room, where she could barely make out a few pieces of furniture in the darkness. It looked to be a meeting area of some sort, with two armchairs in front of a large brown desk. She guessed this was where the undertaker or staff met with grieving family members to comfort and prepare them for the upcoming funeral services.

She retrieved her flashlight from her backpack and clicked it on, looking back through the window to where Leopold was now sitting by his bike on the grass. He hadn't left. She felt relieved. He again gave her a thumbs-up, and she turned back toward the door in the room.

She pulled it open until only a small crack allowed her entry. She clicked on the flashlight to find she was in a long hallway of the business. A velvety green carpet covered the floor, and a soft yellow wallpaper with small green flowers adorned every inch of the walls. Every few feet, a brass lantern jutted out from the wall.

Agatha kept moving to the next room, hoping she wouldn't find herself in an area where they kept the bodies refrigerated or where they burned the bodies. Isn't that what they did when they cremated them? Lit them on fire and watched their skin and organs and bones melt away? She wanted to stay away from that.

The long hallway emptied Agatha Anxious into a large waiting room. A decorative brick fireplace and elaborate mantle were at the far side of the room in front of her. Two large high-backed chairs faced the fireplace, their paw-like, ornate feet grasping the green velvet carpet beneath them.

Agatha sneezed, and her flashlight flickered, slowly diminishing until the room was lit only by the streetlights outside on Howard Avenue. She looked up to see a thin hand extending from one of the chairs. A long, bony finger beckoned her forward.

Agatha reluctantly stepped closer, her heart in her throat, until she stood on the same red rug as the creature. Or person. Mr. Nikolai? Isn't that what Aunt Hattie had called him? Whatever he was.

The finger was long and chalky white. Bone dry. If she touched it, Agatha suspected it would crumble into dust, like the ashes at the end of a cigar. She'd never touch it, of course. And the nail. Long and pointed, just like anyone would imagine an old creature's nails would be. Sandy brown, the color of dirt, or maybe the broth in that soup Agatha's mother made her eat all the time. Her stomach turned at the thought of the soup and the sight of the nail, too.

She took another step forward, and the hand pointed toward the second empty chair next to the fireplace. It then snapped its fingers toward the fireplace, and a small fire partially lit the room. Agatha could see the creature before her. He looked like a very old man. He stood and moved to a corner by the mantle, his movements as fluid as silk in the wind.

"Let me introduce myself, please. I don't want to forget my manners. I am Lucius Nikolai. Lucius Mursadull Nikolai, to be precise. And I am—" He stopped and smiled a villainous half-smile that made Agatha squint. "Well, we will get to that later."

The man's eyes gauged his companion. "Do sit." Agatha said nothing.

"It is not a request."

She moved toward the empty chair in slow motion, keeping the man in her sight. The chair let out a whine under her weight. A plume of dust rose into the air, and she stifled another sneeze. The man, though only a few feet away at the side of the mantle, remained mostly in darkness.

"That's better. I don't get many visitors, so you can imagine how— oh, what's the word—*excited* I am."

Agatha imagined the man was indeed excited but not for any sort of companionship or chat, his enthusiasm instead falling in the hungry category, and she feared she might be his dinner. She checked the time on her watch.

"Let me tell you a little bit about myself, Agatha."

She looked up, startled. "How do you know my name?"

"Because I have been around for a century and a half, that's why. And I have lived in this building for quite a lot of those aforementioned years. You've lived in Biloxi all your young life, have you not?"

"Yes, sir," Agatha said.

The man laughed, and the air suddenly smelled of moldy cheese. Swiss, to be exact.

"No need to call me sir. Although I love formalities, it is not necessary." He paused as he mulled over his next words with great delight. "This is going to be a very informative situation, if you know what I mean."

"I don't...know what you mean." Agatha's voice broke midsentence.

"Correct, so let me finish, and we'll get to that." He smoothed the sides of his hair even though it required no smoothing. His hair was a solid white, nearly the color of his skin. Large black eyes inhabited his eye sockets. No pupil. Other than a light rosy pink on the man's lips, his skin was a light grey with bluish tinges. And it stretched over an angular face, long spindly limbs, and a thin body. He wore a grey waistcoat over a stiff white collared shirt, which was unbuttoned at the neck. Black pants clothed his lower half, and he was wearing a pair of black high-top Converse. They looked brand new.

"You can call me Nikolai. And I've known about you long before you knew about me. I heard you as you rode up on your bicycle, although I knew long before tonight that you'd pay me a visit. Perceivers always need assistance, and I am the one to provide it! I know all that happens here along the Gulf Coast, as it happens, at the precise moment it happens. Which means I know exactly why you are here." Nikolai leaned forward in his chair, making Agatha squirm. "Would you like your precious Auntie back?"

"Yes." She felt tears start to form in her eyes, and she breathed deeply, pushing them away.

"And are you willing to do anything for her?" Agatha took no time to answer. "Yes."

"And what if you don't get her back?" Nikolai smirked, his thin lips spread over their bony canvas.

Agatha was silent. The idea of not having Aunt Hattie back never occurred to her.

Nikolai seemed pleased with Agatha's sorrow, and Agatha decided to change the subject.

"How come you're dressed like that? Especially those shoes." "Have you met many beings like me, young lady?"

"Well, no. But you just said you were extremely old. I figured you would be wearing something more..." Agatha searched for the word.

"Ancient?"

"Yes, ancient. Some stuff with ruffles."

"I actually found these items." Nikolai was stroking the fabric of the waistcoat, caressing it in a way Agatha found uncomfortable. "Well, not *found*. They were left here."

"By who?"

"By two gentlemen who, shall we say, were temporary visitors in my *morgue*," Nikolai emphasized the last word, and Agatha cringed. "Shoes especially are easy to take. Nobody sees a corpse's feet in the casket. Sometimes the shoes don't even fit properly. The feet are curled over and hardened in death, toes frozen in all directions, as was in this particular case. So why waste a perfectly good pair of shoes?" He wiggled his feet to make his point.

Agatha gripped the sides of the chair so tightly that her joints ached, and she shifted her eyes toward the room down the hallway, where only a little while before, she'd entered the funeral home. She estimated it was about five yards away. She wondered if she could make it.

"You cannot," said Nikolai, answering her thoughts. "What?"

"I know what you're asking yourself, and I assure you, you can't make it. Whatever you decide to do, wherever you decide to run, whatever means of escape you're dreaming about, I am faster than you, and I will get there first. It's a waste of time, but go ahead and try it if you must. At least you can tell your friend later, the one out there who is waiting on you-Leopold, isn't it? -that you attempted an escape." His eyes seemed to smile. "If there is a later."

Nikolai sat down and leaned back in his chair, resting his elbows on the arms and touching his fingertips together. He made no effort to get into a ready position. He shifted his weight and crossed one leg over the other. He was getting more comfortable, and Agatha knew he was telling the truth. It was useless. She was wondering why Aunt Hattie ever said Nikolai would be helpful, as he appeared to be more of a threat.

Nikolai's mouth opened slightly, and he wet his thin lips with a reptilian tongue. He straightened the cuffs of his shirt. Agatha's chair suddenly slid across the floor by itself until she was touching knees with him.

She gasped as her heart beat rapidly, a thundering gong with repeated striking, each thud more unsettling than the last. She tried to remind herself to breathe in through her nose and out through her mouth, but the anxiety of the situation trumped each measure she took to calm herself. Her breaths came out in small puffs. She hadn't realized, but her mouth hung wide open, and she was leaning as far back in the crusty chair as she could.

"I'll make you a deal, Agatha Ingrid Anxious. The same deal I give every Perceiver. Listen closely, for I will only say this once." Nikolai's tone was suddenly cold, and his lips curled in a sneer. He leaned forward, his long fingers crawling up Agatha's chair like a spider until his face was close. "You get to ask me three questions. And when I'm done, you'll have all the ammunition you need to continue your quest. I did say this would be informative, didn't I?"

"My...my...quest?" she stammered.

"Yes, your quest," he repeated. "You *are* a Perceiver, aren't you?"

"Yes." Agatha let out her breath through her lips.

He narrowed his eyes at his companion. "Hold out your hand." Agatha did as he commanded, and with the same swift, fluid-like motion from before, Nikolai pricked the tip of one of her fingers in three different places with his fingernail until small

pools of blood formed.

"Ouch!" she jumped back, but Nikolai grasped her wrist, rendering her helpless with his grip.

His solid black eyes held hers as he produced a small glass vial. "Like any good businessman, I do require payment, you know. I help you, and you help me. A taste for a truth." He squeezed her finger until several droplets of blood fell into the vial. Immediately, he brought the container to his lips, his tongue slithering into the bottle until it touched her blood, and he closed his eyes. Then, he corked the top of the vial, smiled, and without hesitation, began. "Are you ready?"

"Yes." Agatha's eyes felt dry. She knew she needed to blink but didn't dare.

"Good. Remember, just three questions, so choose wisely." Nikolai's chair was suddenly empty, and he now stood at the fireplace, his back to her. He cleared his throat, arched his long, thin spine, each vertebra coming into alignment until he seemed much taller than before, and he straightened his shirt as if on stage, about to give the greatest performance of his life. He slowly turned to face Agatha and gave her an unnerving smile that oozed pure hunger. A long overdue type of hunger, Agatha thought, like starvation.

She now saw Nikolai's gums were black, and for the first time, she saw his teeth, which were a perfect arrangement of flawless little marshmallows. They had a childlike quality about them. They seemed too small, and there were far too many of them. Small pellets of sweat peppered Agatha's forehead.

Nikolai gave two loud claps of his hands, and the room went dark. Agatha kept her eyes wide though she couldn't see, the fire no longer burning in the fireplace. For a moment, nothing. No sound. No movement. Anticipation weighted the air like an anchor. She wondered if Leopold was still outside waiting for her. She longed to scream his name, but would he hear her?

Suddenly, from the darkness to Agatha's left, and much closer than she would have liked, was a giggle. Before she could gasp, a cold hand covered her mouth, the ashen fingers clamping down one by one in a choreographed dance against her lips, pressing her head back against the chair.

Nikolai's tongue brushed Agatha's ear, and he spoke in a whisper that was more of a hiss. "Let us begin, shall we?"

CHAPTER 20
STAY THE COURSE

Before she knew it, Lucius Nikolai was seated back in his chair across from Agatha, one leg crossed over the other, the Converse-clad foot bouncing happily on top of the

opposite leg's knee. He smiled at Agatha, eagerly awaiting her first question.

She touched her ear, half expecting to find ashy bits, a powdery substance, or skin crumbs of some sort leftover from Lucius Nikolai having touched her. Her hand came away clean. She glanced down the long green hallway, the wall sconces now lit with small flickering flames.

"He's still waiting for you," Nikolai said, referring to Leopold.

Agatha nodded. She tried to clear her mind of a few things since it was becoming increasingly apparent Nikolai could either read her mind or see her thoughts. She did not care to give him the satisfaction of showing any fear. Just three questions. Her blood for three truths he would tell her. How could she decide?

She decided to start with her most pressing one. "Where is Aunt Hattie?" she blurted out before properly formulating the question in her mind. She regretted it instantly. She'd hoped to fashion a three-part question—one of those Mrs. Wright often talked about—that required several answers even though it was only a single question.

"At Doom's Maskerades," Nikolai giggled, pressing his fingertips together but keeping his eyes on Agatha. He said no more than those three words and seemed quite pleased with himself at having to give no further explanation.

"That's not fair," said Agatha. "I KNOW she's at that mask shop. That's not what I meant!"

"Two questions left." Nikolai sneered, undeterred, tapping his fingertips together.

Agatha pursed her lips together. *This is a game, and he's cheating.* She squeezed her eyes closed, thinking hard on her next question—no more missteps.

"Who has my Aunt Hattie?" she said, finally opening her eyes and staring down the old creature opposite her.

Nikolai uncrossed his legs, planting both of his feet on the floor, and put his hands on his lap. "The Woman in White." He was still pleased with himself.

Agatha knew exactly what he meant, and he was still cheating. "What you mean to say is that Blanche Caillavet—or her ghost—is The Woman in White."

"Is that your final question?" Nikolai asked.

"No!" Agatha screamed. "Don't you dare. That was a statement, not a question, and you know it!"

Nikolai let out a laugh that was more of a rusty, dry cough, and Agatha could smell his breath from her chair. She turned away.

After a few minutes of silence, Nikolai cleared his throat. "I'm waiting. I don't have all night, you know. I do have other more pressing—"

"How do I defeat The Woman in White?" Agatha interrupted him, at last exhausted of his games.

"Ahhh," Nikolai stood and leaned against the fireplace. "At last! A proper question worth answering. Now we're getting somewhere, Agatha Anxious. Too bad for you. It's your final question and not your first." He ran his tongue over his teeth, its forked end peeking out between his parted lips. He paused momentarily as if deciding the best way to form his response and thus, cheat Agatha out of a proper explanation.

She knew what he was doing and narrowed her eyes at him. "Have you seen The Woman in White yet?" Nikolai began. "No," she said.

"Well, when you do, you'll understand. Back in the 1930s, in the prime of her life, Blanche Caillavet was quite the looker, if you know what I mean."

Agatha thought for a moment. "Beautiful."

"You could say that, yes—the envy of many ladies here on the Gulf Coast. I quite admired her myself, you know. The beauty of that caliber doesn't happen often." Nikolai faced the fireplace, rubbing one hand back and forth over his chin. "And usually, that kind of beauty comes with a large ego."

He turned to Agatha and placed both hands on the arms of her chair, leaning his face close to hers until his solid black eyes were just inches away. He blinked, and she saw a gel-like coating wash over them, like a second skin. *A second pair of eyelids,* she thought.

"What I'm getting at, Miss Anxious is that death isn't so pretty or kind or sweet. And mark my words, Blanche Caillavet doesn't exactly like the look of herself these days."

Agatha wasn't sure what he meant. Nikolai returned to his seat across from her, still stroking his pointy, white chin. He blinked again before holding up a long, thin finger.

"Now that you've asked your three questions, a question and a warning before you leave, Agatha Anxious. What is your mission, as you see it now?"

Agatha did not hesitate. "To get Aunt Hattie back."

"Wrong!" Nikolai laughed. "Think harder. You had a mission long before that. What was it? Or *who* was it for, rather?"

Agatha thought for a moment. Nothing in the world was more important to her than saving her aunt. She thought back over the past few days' occurrences. What was he referring to?

Seeing her distress, Nikolai smiled, displaying his perfect marshmallow teeth again. "Let me help you. What ghost were you helping first?"

The ghost. Her original ghost.

"The one who wants his coin back."

"Correct!" Nikolai clapped. "And that, my dear, is ALL you are to do. Do you understand?"

Agatha was indignant. She stood up. "Do you mean to say I'm to help this dumb ghost with his coin and totally forget about Aunt Hattie?" Her voice was higher than she expected.

"Dumb ghost?" Nikolai rolled his eyes and pointed to the chair. "Oh, sit down."

Agatha sat.

"And by the way, yes," he smiled again. "What has happened to your aunt is merely a distraction, Agatha. The Woman in White doesn't want you helping other ghosts, you see. And she's more powerful because of it. The less you help other ghosts, the more powerful she is. The more you help other ghosts, the weaker she is. It's that simple. For the foreseeable future, you will need to forget about your aunt and focus on your five."

Agatha couldn't believe her ears. How could she ignore the fact that something had happened to her aunt and she wasn't supposed to do anything about it? This was absurd.

"My five? What does that mean?"

Lucius Nikolai licked his lips. "Is this another question?" He waved a lone finger in her direction. "Another small taste for another truth, my dear."

Without hesitation, Agatha jammed her open palm to him and looked away. He opened the vial and chose another finger this time.

"Five ghosts, Agatha Anxious. Five Deadfellows will need your help before you can put Ms. Caillavet back in her crypt forever," Nikolai said, wiping his mouth.

Agatha stayed silent. She felt woozy but kept her eyes open wide to pay attention.

"Every Perceiver is assigned Deadfellows, and that's what you're doing, isn't it? Helping the dead? Some Perceivers are assigned two. Some, twelve. You, my lovely, will have five." He drummed his fingers on the arm of his chair, staring intently into what felt like Agatha's soul.

"It was determined long ago. Fate, let's call it."

"How....do you...know all of...this?" she mumbled, struggling with the words.

"Anyway," he continued, ignoring her. "Your aunt is merely a distraction. To steer you off course. I'm not saying you won't get her back. But then again, I'm not saying you will, either. I have nothing to do with any of that. I provide assistance but do not interfere. Just remember: A distraction."

After a pause, he leaned in near for the third time, and she held her breath to avoid Nikolai's stench. "Stay the course, Agatha. You have a duty," he whispered. "Focus on your five."

Suddenly, three loud knocks were at the front door. Nikolai disappeared momentarily, but Agatha could still feel his presence. She exhaled. Leopold hadn't forgotten her.

Nikolai stepped forth from the darkest corner of the room, his hands on his hips. "Well, well. Just in time. Let's let your friend in, shall we?" He pointed a long, chalky finger toward the front door, and it swung open at his command. There stood Leopold, his fist still raised in the knocking position, as he came face to face with Lucius Nikolai, who was now at the funeral home's entrance.

Nikolai placed his thin palms on Leopold's shoulders, lifting him off the ground with no effort, and in one brisk movement, placed him in the chair opposite Agatha. "Do come in, Mr. Panic."

Leopold curled himself into a ball, pulling his knees to his chest, and faced away from Nikolai to avoid his glare.

Agatha's mouth fell open, snapping out of her daze. "You can see him?" she asked Leopold.

Lucius Nikolai cocked his head back and laughed. "Of course, he can see me. Did you not know? He is a Perceiver too."

CHAPTER 21
A REVELATION

O nce Nikolai let them go—he'd even blown a kiss and waved his spindly fingers goodbye in a last gesture of sarcasm—Agatha and Leopold gathered their bikes

and stood on the deserted Howard Avenue, breathing in the evening's sticky air. Feeling dizzy, Agatha sat on the curb and rubbed her forehead. She felt no more informed or further along in her journey than when she'd entered the Benford-O'Malley Funeral Home.

"Agatha?" she heard Leopold say in between groggy, mismatched thoughts. "We really need to go."

"I only need a minute," she mumbled, her hands still on her temples.

"It's been thirty!" he exclaimed in a whisper. "We don't want to get caught out here."

Thirty minutes? How had thirty minutes passed? She still felt groggy. What had Lucius done to her?

He can be dangerous; you must know that. She heard Aunt Hattie's words bobbing around in her brain like ice in a punch bowl. *He always asks for something from you, so be prepared to give.*

Her blood. That's what she'd given him. And it had momentarily weakened her, made her lightheaded and sleepy.

She mustered the strength to get to her feet, gripped the bike's rusty handlebars, and glanced at her watch. It was nearing midnight. Unsure of what to do next, as she hadn't set up any real overnight plans with anyone, she headed back toward the cemetery, Leopold following silently behind her. Again, they took the backroads, finally turning onto Gill Avenue, where they parked the bikes in Leopold's carport where they'd been just hours before.

They stood in the carport for a while, not speaking to each other, Leopold pretending to tie a shoelace that wasn't undone in the first place.

"Why didn't you tell me?" Agatha finally broke the silence.

"I did, though, didn't I?" Leopold stood and stuffed his hands in the pockets of his jeans. He stared at her—hard—with a pleading sort of look. "I told you my dead grandfather sits on my bed and talks to me. Practically all the time. And he's dead. Wasn't that sort of a hint that I was seeing dead people?"

He wasn't wrong. He had told her, in a way.

"I guess," she said, biting her lip. "I just didn't realize."

"I mean, I didn't know there were words for it. Like, Perceiver. Or whatever that old man said," he continued. "But I've seen things I probably shouldn't have seen. I came to you that day in the cemetery because I didn't know what to do about it. I hate this." He paused, sifting through words in his mind and choosing them carefully. "I thought you could...help me."

Agatha looked down at her shoes, some of the tape breaking away from the rest of the shoe, splintering in different directions like five fingers of a hand. She scuffed it against the pavement. A small ball of something formed in her stomach, but this time it wasn't nausea. It felt very much like regret. And shame. She'd overlooked Leopold's asking for help because she'd been so consumed. With what? Dresses and patterns and homework and book reports. *He even switched book reports with you, Agatha. Practically wrote it for you!*

Her brain pounded inside her skull, and she closed her eyes. "Maybe we can help each other," she spoke in nearly a whisper. She looked up at him, her brown eyes catching his. "I have something I need to do, and I'm scared."

He nodded.

"And also, I'm sorry."

The corners of his mouth turned up into a smile, but he turned away to hide it. "You're not going to hug me or anything, are you? Because I uh, I don't do hugs," Leopold said, still facing away from her.

He sounded very much like he wanted a hug, Agatha thought. But no, she had no intention of giving him a hug. The apology had been enough. Sometimes those two little *I'm sorry* words were the hardest thing to say.

"No way," she said. "I don't do mushy stuff."

He gave her a thumbs-up, and it reminded her of the one he'd given her at the funeral home. Thinking of Lucius Nikolai irritated her. "So, I didn't make any plans to stay anywhere tonight. Well, actually, I told my parents I was staying at Tippy's, but I can't go over there now. And I can't really go home," she said, motioning toward his carport. "Mind if I sleep in the corner over there by the bikes? I'll be gone in just a few hours."

"Um, ok. Do you need a blanket or anything?"

She shook her head. "Nah. I probably won't even sleep, really."

"Ok," he said, uneasy. He started toward the back door of the home and stopped. "You know, I would invite you in, but uh, my mother should be home by now, so..." he trailed off.

"What about your dad? Is your dad here too?" she blurted out, intentionally being nosy.

Leopold paused. "No. Just my mom."

He continued walking toward the house, his hands in his pockets, and when he was nearly out of Agatha's view, he called back to her, "My dad doesn't live with us if that's what you're asking. He's dead too."

Agatha grimaced and slapped her palm against her forehead. Why did she have to ask? It was none of her business. She plopped her backpack on the ground in the corner of the carport and sat down next to it when she saw Leopold's face peer around the corner, a smile spreading across his pink lips.

"I'm kidding. He's alive. But he doesn't live with us. Stop being nosy, Agatha." He winked at her and, with that, disappeared around the corner.

AGATHA FELT the sunlight from behind her closed eyes, her eyeballs dry from a heavy sleep. She opened them to find she had indeed fallen asleep in an upright position, her arms propped up on her backpack, which was in her lap. She didn't remember placing her bag there, but then again, she didn't recall falling asleep either.

She checked her watch. 7:03. Good. She could take her time. Arriving right around 8:00 a.m. would probably be best. Right as her parents were getting up for the day and wouldn't be thinking of calling Tippy's house to check on her.

She was yawning as she heard a door open from behind Leopold's house. An old, rusty whining creak. There must be a screen door or a porch back there, she thought. Maybe he was coming to check on her. She looked down at her dress, smoothing out the wrinkled fabric and checking her hair with her hands. It was wonky, as usual.

There was a pause after the screen door slammed against its frame, and then a couple of slow, drawn-out footsteps down what she imagined were a couple of stairs. The footsteps got louder, and they seemed to head in her direction, but the gait was different. Leopold was light on his feet. Waiflike. He was thin and tall and barely made any noise when he walked. And when he did, his steps were quick and fast, indicative of his nervous nature—like Agatha's

This person-whoever it was-was slow and heavy, and the footsteps were uneven. A step and then a scuff, as if they were dragging something behind them. A leg, perhaps? Leopold said his dad didn't live there.

Agatha lay flat on her stomach and squirmed her way to the other side of the one car parked in the carport until the car was between her and whoever was about to appear behind the corner. Although, she already knew who it was. Only one person walked like that. Only one person in the world, dragging a heavy leg slightly behind them. She would know their lumbering gait anywhere.

From beneath the car, she saw the two brown boots walk past her, down the driveway, and take a left onto Gill Avenue, heading toward the beach. Once the person was down the street, Agatha moved into a crouching position and peered from behind the carport's wall. She couldn't believe her eyes.

It was Mr. Dominicus, and she scolded herself for not knowing. For being mean and irritable and rude to Leopold about it. And everything else she'd been in between. Inconsiderate. Unthoughtful. Consumed with herself and her problems, and altogether not a good friend.

She watched the figure take a right on Beach Boulevard, heading toward the only place in the world she imagined he would be going: her Aunt Hattie's shop.

She grabbed her backpack and sprinted toward home, her stomach wanting to heave with the sickening revelation: *Mr. Dominicus was Leopold's dead grandfather.*

CHAPTER 22
THE NECESSARY ASSISTANCE OF DORIAN DOOM

Monday morning dawned, and still no Aunt Hattie. Her parents were in a frenzy, but Agatha, still unable to tell them the truth, was unafraid. She remained steadfast in her mission, and she knew exactly what she needed to do, although she was still unsure how to go about doing it. She planned to corner Dorian Doom during lunch.

She met Leopold in the cemetery, and they walked to school nervously, her biting her nails, him messing with a piece of hair, constantly tucking it behind his ear.

"Did you finish the book report?" he asked her to make conversation.

"I saw your grandfather yesterday," she retorted, ignoring him.

He dropped his hand from his hair. "Which means I don't have to tell you why I left your aunt's shop that day, then?"

"Which means you don't have to tell me why you left my aunt's shop that day, then," Agatha repeated. "I guess you didn't know he works for my aunt."

Leopold snorted. "I mean, can you really work for someone when you're dead?"

Agatha stopped in the middle of the sidewalk. She hadn't thought about it that way before. "Well, I guess not. I don't think Aunt Hattie actually pays him. He sort of volunteers? Can you even call it that? Can you volunteer when you're dead?"

Leopold shrugged. "Gives him something to do, I guess. He probably is there all the time because I guess your aunt is a Perceiver, and he knows that and feels comfortable."

Agatha nodded, a realization washing over her. *And Aunt Hattie knew I was a Perceiver because I saw Mr. Dominicus.* She shook her head. So many questions for Aunt Hattie now, and no Aunt Hattie to answer them. She felt a pain in her heart.

They spent the rest of their walk to school joking about Mr. Dominicus. It felt good to laugh, and she could tell it was good for Leopold too. Perhaps he could stop being afraid of his grandfather.

She turned to Leopold before heading to her locker. "Meet me at my uncle's grave after school. I know what I need to do to get Aunt Hattie back. Nikolai wasn't totally useless," she snorted. "But I need to enlist someone else's help, too."

Leopold pointed to himself, his finger on his chest.

"You and someone else," she started down the hallway. "Dorian Doom."

IN HISTORY CLASS, Mr. Barone—whose tie choice was a solid orange—handed out a surprise quiz, but Agatha didn't mind. Her thoughts were on other things. She snuck as many glimpses of Dorian as she could, trying to gauge his mood. He appeared pretty happy, joking with a few of his friends. She half hoped to see him toying with something in his pocket as if the coin had magically been found and she wouldn't have to make an excursion to the mask shop.

No such luck.

As the bell rang, she scribbled something on a piece of torn paper and, gathering her nerve, dropped it on Dorian's desk as she exited the classroom. She didn't look back to see if he'd gotten it. She just hoped luck was on her side, even though Mr. Barone said there was no such thing as luck.

After school, she nearly ran the whole way to the cemetery, arriving first at her uncle's grave. Throwing aside her backpack, she sat down on the cool marble footstone and checked her watch. Leopold arrived shortly after, asking no questions, and instead took his place beside her on the ground.

Fifteen minutes later, and much to her relief, Dorian Doom rounded the corner, a look of confusion on his face. He wrinkled his forehead as he approached them, a look that was meant to convey aggravation but appeared more smoldering and mysterious to Agatha. She felt her heart skip another beat and shook it off. She had things to do.

"Meet me in the cemetery after school?" Dorian asked, pointing to Agatha's crumbled piece of paper. "Ok. I'm here. And I missed my bus for this. Now what?"

He scanned the open field of gravestones as if making sure no one was watching them. He rocked back and forth on the balls of his feet, his hands jammed deep into his pockets, and Agatha wondered if this was what he did when he was nervous. It seemed each one of her friends had a nervous tick. Leopold with his hair twirling. She with her nail-biting. Perhaps this was Dorian's. Agatha wasted no time. "I need to get into your mask shop tonight. And the only person to help me do that is you." She stood tall, staring Dorian in his eyes, daring him to say no.

Dorian sighed. "Are you out of your mind? I told you, bad—"

"Things happen there at night." Agatha finished the sentence for him. Dorian looked at her.

"Listen, my aunt disappeared there a couple of days ago and.."

"Wait, what?!" Dorian stepped back.

"Let me finish!" Agatha insisted. "None of this is going to make sense to you, but let me finish. My aunt went there the other night to get that coin of yours. It was the last place she went, and now she's gone. Her truck was found abandoned in Vieux Marche near the Golden Fisherman, and I know she went into that mask shop. And I know something happened there with Blanche Caillavet."

She saw Dorian swallow at the mention of the name, his face paler than before.

"The Woman in White," he said softly.

"Yes, the Woman in White. And I know you know what I'm talking about. Have you seen her?"

Dorian threw off his backpack and sat on the ground, his head now in his hands. For a few moments, he said nothing. Agatha looked at Leopold, who smoothed a few strands of hair behind his ear.

"Just the smallest glimpse," Dorian said, barely audible. "I saw what I think was her—one evening when I was closing up. And I've never stayed late there again. Ever."

He looked over at Leopold and then back at Agatha and suddenly threw his backpack over one shoulder. Dorian turned to leave but muttered the only words Agatha needed to hear. "I can get you in, but I'm not going in with you. I'll leave the key hidden under the mat at the shop's door after my shift this afternoon. Give it back to me tomorrow at school."

After walking a few steps away, Dorian turned back to both of his classmates. "Oh, and we never had this conversation."

CHAPTER 23
AN OLD PHOTOGRAPH

The plan was simple. Pretend to go to bed and then sneak out, meeting Leopold at his house. Then, together they would head to the mask shop, where Dorian hopefully

made good on his word by leaving the key under the door's mat. *But of course, nothing goes as planned when one needs it to,* Agatha thought. She preferred to be pessimistic than optimistic. Pessimists were never disappointed.

Agatha pretended to be sleepy earlier than usual that evening, and she was in bed a full thirty minutes before her normal bedtime, but that didn't usher her parents to bed as she had hoped. She could hear them talking at the dining room table, playing a game of chess—of all games, chess lasted forever—until nearly 10 p.m.

Good thing she'd told Leopold to wait for her no matter what. Not that Leopold had the nerve to go to the mask shop without her. That would never happen. Agatha lay in her bed smiling. She seemed to be the bravest of all her friends, and most of her friends were boys. She was pleased. Aunt Hattie would be, too.

When she finally heard her parents' footfalls in the hallway and their nightly routine being finished—teeth brushing, toilet flushing, and finally the click of their bedside lamps—Agatha waited another twenty minutes just to be certain they were in the midst of deep sleep before she tiptoed across her room and threw on a black dress with black stockings.

The color of stealth, she thought to herself. Again, she smiled.

She felt like a ninja.

She glanced over at the Scrabble board, still bearing one of the ghost's first communications with her. She wondered if he liked to communicate differently each time. He hadn't touched the Scrabble board since. Gently, she removed the twelve letters and selected a few others. She wasn't sure he would see her message but had an inkling he might. In any case, she needed the ghost to know something.

One by one, she laid her selected tiles back on the board, this time in a vertical line. A few of the letters didn't fit on the board, but she set them right beneath the others on the desk. Once finished, she stepped back and admired her work. More of a mantra for herself than a message for the Deer Island Ghost. But she still hoped he would see it. She read it three times aloud, feeling more and more at ease each time the words passed from her lips.

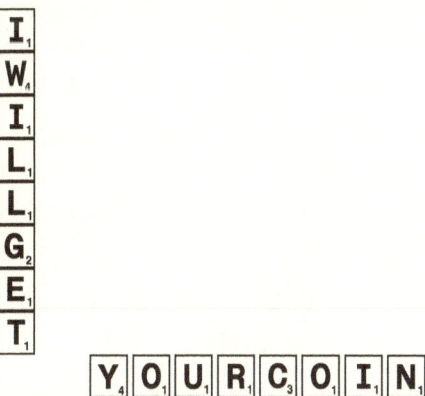

She navigated the wooden floorboards in the hallway and living room to avoid the creaky ones and soon found herself facing the back door. She'd chosen the back door instead of the front one because it seemed to be far less creaky and also was farthest away from her parent's room. Macbeth followed her, letting out a small whine or two to inform her of his concern. She knelt down and buried her face in his black fur, wrapping her arms around him in a tight hug, where she stayed for one long, silent minute. He let her.

She rubbed his ears—his favorite spot—and whispered into one of them, "I'll be back shortly, boy."

Gripping the brass handle, she took a breath and turned, opening the door only as far as necessary and slipping out. Once it closed behind her, she waited another five minutes just to be sure she heard no sound from inside the house.

Silence.

She slipped on her shoes and ran all the way to Leopold's, hoping he hadn't fallen asleep. Once she arrived, she saw the light in his bedroom—good old Leopold. He really is a good friend, she thought to herself.

She knocked on his window three times and waited. He appeared outside a few minutes later, a fanny pack around his waist. She giggled and pointed. "What is that?"

"My flashlight fits in here," he said, adjusting it. "What?"

She shook her head. "Never mind." He was far more prepared than she was, as she'd left her flashlight on her desk.

Agatha held up her hand. "Wait. I have a question." "What?"

"Did you finish your book report?" "My book report?" he asked, surprised.

"Yeah," she said. "The one I asked you to switch with me." "Yes. Why? You want that one too?" he smiled at her, exposing his wayward front tooth.

Agatha rolled her eyes. "No. But I do want to know where you got your information on Blanche Caillavet."

Leopold shrugged his shoulders. "I dunno. Some book I checked out from the library."

"Do you still have it?"

"Yes. In my room." Leopold pointed at his window. "Listen, are we going to do this or not? I'd like to get this over with. I do want to live past tonight, you know."

"Go get it." "What?"

Agatha stamped her foot. "Just get it!" she said in the highest whisper she could manage, hoping to convey a sense of urgency to Leopold. "I'll explain later."

Leopold did as he was told and reappeared moments later with another tattered hardback that looked very much like the one he'd given her at the library. *Biloxi Library needs to update some of its research materials,* she thought to herself. She threw the book in her backpack without looking at its cover.

"Ready?" she said, determination washing over her. He nodded.

They grabbed the same bikes and used the same back roads as before. Their ride was silent, partly due to the late hour but mostly because of the nerves that neither wanted to admit to having.

They arrived in Vieux Marche a short time later and parked their bikes at the business across from Doom's Maskerades. The streetlights lit up the Golden Fisherman, whose outstretched hands begged ominously for their company.

Agatha sat under the business's grey awning. Leopold squatted beside her as she removed the book from her bag, squinting to read the torn cover. *A History of Mardi Gras in Biloxi.* She turned to Leopold.

"Oh. So, this isn't about her death or ghost or anything like that?"

He shook his head. "No, I added a few bits and pieces at the end of my book report, but I focused mostly on the Mardi Gras aspect. I mean, that was practically her whole life. It was all she cared about."

Agatha flipped through the pages, her fingers finally coming to rest on a couple of dogeared pages. She opened the book wide to discover a full-page black and white portrait of a woman who peered at the camera from over her left shoulder, several long blonde curls draped down her back. The rest of her hair was swept upwards atop her head in more curls, where it was fastened with pins made of pearls and flowers.

A matching pearl necklace hung daintily from her thin neck. Light-colored eyes, perhaps blue or green, beset with long and lush eyelashes, stared at Agatha from the page. The woman's skin was flawless and smooth, noticeable even to the viewer of a photograph many decades old. A pair of plump, petite lips curled in a shy smile completed the young, feminine face.

She was the very definition of class, luxury, and wealth. Beneath the photograph, a caption read: Blanche N. Caillavet, 1933.

"So, four years before she became a Mardi Gras Queen," Agatha said. Lucius Nikolai was right. She was stunning.

"Yeah, well, apparently that ruined her life. Or something did," Leopold broke into her thoughts as she stared at the picture. "Turn the page."

Agatha did and was faced with a much different photograph. An older, greyer Blanche Caillavet stared outward from the book. More wrinkles and many more years. Still, the same woman, although something had changed. Agatha noticed the same flawless skin, the same upper-class dress, and the same air of wealth and superiority. But her eyes were different.

These two eyes stared Agatha down from inside the book, full of something much darker than the picture on the previous page. This version of Blanche Caillavet seemed exhausted and unwell, as if she were drained of something. Or she was maybe carrying something. *The weight of something*, Agatha thought. It looked very much like worry. And suffering. This woman wasn't smiling. Beyond her sickly look, she seemed determined about something. She displayed a resolve that was almost...evil.

Agatha flipped back to the first picture and abruptly ripped it out.

"Hey!" Leopold shouted. "I have to turn that book back into the library."

"They won't even notice," Agatha said, brushing past him and crossing the street to the mask shop. She knelt by the mat and held her breath, hoping Dorian had done what he said he would do. She didn't want to throw a rock into the shop's front window, but she would if she had to.

She peeled back the mat to reveal a single silver skeleton key.

Perfect.

"Agatha, what if I have to pay for that book?" Leopold was now beside her, twirling his hair as if the library charging him money for the book was their greatest concern at the moment.

"I need that picture, Leopold. It's my—" she fumbled for the word. "My weapon."

Agatha faced the front of the shop again, folding the photograph into fours and tucking it into the side of her shoe. Thanks, mom, for no pockets, she silently scolded her mother. And then she placed the skeleton key in the lock and turned.

"Apparently," Agatha said, quoting an old creature who'd been moderately helpful, "Blanche Caillavet doesn't like the look of herself these days."

CHAPTER 24
A RIDDLE FOR YOUR AUNTIE

O nce inside Doom's Maskerades, the door quietly closed behind them. Agatha faced the same long aisle her aunt had seen a few nights before. The mirrored walls and masks of all different colors, fabrics, materials, and faces. She shuddered. If she never saw another Mardi Gras mask in her life, she'd be pleased.

A lone white cat came bounding down the aisle toward Agatha, immediately rubbing itself against her legs, butting its head into her shins. It twirled itself around her ankles and pawed at her stockings.

"Geez, it really likes you," Leopold whispered to Agatha.

Agatha was surprised Leopold decided to accompany her into the shop, although he told her he would stay by the front door to be a lookout instead of venturing into the back of the shop where Agatha seemed determined to go.

Agatha patted the cat's head. "Where'd you come from? I guess this place can't be all that bad if you're living here, huh?"

The cat reminded her of the ones Aunt Hattie took care of, and she wondered if those cats had found another home in the last few days. Her heart sunk. If so, the new caretaker surely wasn't doing as good a job as Aunt Hattie.

She stepped forward cautiously, her taped shoes scuffing against a few of the wooden floorboards that creaked under her weight. The cat ran in front of her, abruptly stopping in her path. Agatha shooed it away and tried to take a few more steps, but again, the cat placed itself in front of her shoes as if deliberately trying to prevent her from walking, again winding itself in and out of her legs.

The cat stared at her, its brown eyes sending her a warning. Agatha realized she'd never seen a white cat with brown eyes. Just green. Or blue. She again shooed it away, and finally, a loud stamp of her foot sent it running into the darkness near the black velvet curtain at the end of the aisle.

Agatha remembered Dorian referring to the back room of the shop, precisely where he'd lost his coin and refused to go find it. She found herself standing in front of the curtain, staring at an elaborate mask encased in glass in the corner. The white cat pawed her foot to get her attention, and she could see its fur moving and realized it was trembling.

Agatha reached up and felt the curtain against her fingertips. She glanced behind her at Leopold, who was biting his nails, standing tall and firm in his position by the front door. *Ready to turn and run at any moment*, she thought. She smirked, never having seen Leopold bite his nails.

Agatha cleared her throat, summoning a few brief flashes of courage, and whispered into the curtain, "Aunt Hattie?"

For a long, eternal moment, there was no sound. Just the creak of the floor beneath Agatha's feet as she swayed, unsteady in her small shoes. Then, she heard a soft whimper from behind the curtain, a low, sad combination of sounds, drawn-out and separated by sniffles. Someone was weeping.

"Auntie?" she repeated, her hand now on the curtain, ready to yank it open but unsure what she would find lurking behind it. "Miss Magnolia?" the voice managed to say in between small
sobs.

Agatha's heart skipped a beat, and she looked back at Leopold, who firmly shook his head back and forth. He'd heard it too. He'd only met her aunt once, but he'd caught it. Aunt Hattie would've said, "Miz." This wasn't Aunt Hattie.

Agatha grasped both sides of the curtain and threw them open in either direction from the middle. She gritted her teeth, ready to stare down whatever creature or ghost she would find in the back room of the shop. But she was ill-prepared for what she saw.

An old woman, very much like the second photograph in Leopold's book, floated before her, just a couple inches off the ground and a few feet away. Her long-sleeve, white lace gown covered nearly every inch of her body from her neck to her wrists to her ankles, and the bottom ends of the dress bore brown stains and splotches that Aunt Hattie would've most definitely identified as cemetery mud. Agatha was sure this was her coffin attire.

The woman moved a few inches closer, her stiff, pointed toes dragging against the wooden floor of the mask shop in slow motion. The woman's head hung low and out front due to the severe curvature of her back. If she'd been alive and walking, she would've used a cane. The person floating before Agatha, however, was neither walking nor alive.

But she was most definitely Blanche Caillavet.

As she moved closer, Agatha saw her grey hair was coiffed in a fancy bun atop her head; several long tendrils fell around her ears and neck like silvery snakes. Patches of bruised skin adorned her forehead and cheeks, with some of the skin cracked and falling away around her mouth. For the first time, Blanche looked up, cocking her head sideways, and Agatha stared into the dead face.

Grey skin and thick black rims framed a pair of yellow irises.

The woman smiled and then let out a snicker as if she found the sight of Agatha Anxious amusing. Agatha saw black spaces in between her teeth, indicative of the rot that came with death.

Agatha heard Leopold gasp behind her but couldn't—and wouldn't—take her eyes off the woman.

"Well, well," The Woman in White finally said, a husky, smoke-laden voice, much deeper than Agatha expected, her vocal cords as dried and cracked as her skin. She arched her back and appeared straighter than before, her feet still a couple of inches above the floor. Her long thin arms appeared from behind her back, the frail, gangly fingers with grey nails indicative of an elderly person. She held two items.

"Are you looking for this?" she hissed.

In her right hand, she held Dorian's coin. She moved it between her thin fingers seamlessly, as if showing Agatha a magic trick. In her other hand was a silver Mardi Gras mask shaped like a cat, elaborate with glitter, diamonds, crystals, whiskers, red ribbons, and black lips. It was an exact copy of the one in the glass case, and it scowled at Agatha.

Agatha swallowed. "I want my Aunt Hattie back," she said firmly, pretending that was her only objective.

The old woman threw her head back at an unnatural angle and laughed, several small vertebrae poking through the thin skin of her neck. "Ahhh. I'm afraid your aunt is quite different, now," she said, her yellow eyes looking down toward the bottom of the velvet curtain by Agatha's feet.

Agatha followed her gaze until her eyes rested on the white cat with brown eyes. Agatha now saw the chest of a cat had a design just like the ones at Aunt Hattie's house. But this one was different. Agatha gasped.

It was a black spiral, exactly like Aunt Hattie's necklace.

Agatha turned to the old woman and gritted her teeth. "What have you done!" she screamed.

Blanche Caillavet let out a cackle. "If you'd like your Auntie back, you'll have to try on this." She thrust the cat mask forward, her toes dragging across the floor a few more inches toward Agatha.

Agatha stepped back, and the old woman abruptly stopped, snatching her arm back until she remained on the other side of the curtain. Agatha looked around and realized she was fully in the sales area of the shop. The area with masks and mirrors and glass cases.

Mirrors.

Agatha focused her eyes on the old woman. Of course. Mirrors. Here, Aunt Hattie's room, on the doors of Aunt Hattie's shop. Everywhere. They kept Blanche Caillavet enclosed, didn't they? Contained because she couldn't bear her reflection. Which means she couldn't leave the back part of the mask shop. And her aunt surrounded herself with mirrors as protection in case the old woman ever did.

Agatha stepped partially into the shop's backroom.

The old woman stared at Agatha, her yellow eyes wide and her dry mouth slightly ajar. "You do want to see your Auntie again, don't you?" She backed up a few inches, keeping her eyes on Agatha. She licked her dry lips and began:

> *I do not have a body, but I have a tail and head.*
> *I belong to someone dead. What am I?*

She clapped her hands, applauding herself and pretending to take a curtsy while waiting for an answer from Agatha, who stood silent.

A riddle. Leopold had said so, hadn't he? *'A riddle she'll ask to sell you a mask. Yourself and your soul are the debt.'* Agatha hated riddles.

"You have no answer?" she asked huskily.

"The answer is a coin," Agatha said, keeping her eyes on the woman.

"Correct! And it looks like it's worth a great deal. But is it worth your aunt? You can trade it in for her, you know." The old woman shrugged her bony shoulders, pleased.

Agatha heard Lucius Nikolai in her head. *Your aunt is merely a distraction. Stay the course.* He'd been right. The Woman in White wanted nothing more than to stop her from assisting the Deer Island Ghost just so she could become more powerful. But the idea of turning down the opportunity to have Aunt Hattie back overwhelmed Agatha.

Stay the course.

"No," Agatha gritted her teeth. Never in her life had the word been so difficult to say. And painful.

"Well then, your only other option is wearing my mask if you want to see your Auntie again," she said, gripping it with her thin, knobby hand and floating forward until she was only inches from Agatha's face. "Let me place it on you."

Agatha felt the red ribbons brush the side of her head. Anger filled her, and she saw a flash of white followed by stars and glitter in front of her eyes. Blanche Caillavet and her stupid riddles. Stealing her Auntie and then giving her ridiculous choices where neither outcome would be good. Who knew if she'd give her Aunt Hattie back, anyway?

Agatha's heart pounded in her chest as she threw herself forward, slapping the mask from the old woman's hands as hard as she could. It flew in the direction of the white cat, who now pounced forward, leaping toward the ghastly woman's other hand, which held the coin.

Blanche Caillavet let out a sound that was more of a growl than a scream, and the coin hit the wooden floor, rolling down the aisle toward Leopold, who picked it up as quickly as he could.

Agatha pulled the folded photograph from her shoe and thrust it forward. "How do you like yourself now?" she screamed, holding it in Blanche Caillavet's face.

The old woman's yellow eyes shut when she saw the picture, and she winced as if wounded by the sight of herself. She snarled and gnashed her teeth, finally exposing all of them, some coated in a dark slime that now dripped from her lips. "I will get you, Agatha Anxious!" she said in a sneer, shaking her head violently until all her hair fell in long silvery snake-like curls around her face. Some of it fell from her head onto the floor. She tore at her dress with her pointed fingernails and wailed.

Agatha fell backward onto the wood floor and scrambled toward Leopold, who held out his hand, pulling her to her feet. Leopold threw open the door and forced Agatha out.

"No!" she cried. "The cat!"

"It's too late!" Leopold screamed, pushing her through the doorway.

Agatha gripped the door with both hands, looking back once more down the shop's aisle. She saw the cat by the velvet curtain, its hind fur ruffled and uneven, its tail whipping and flicking angrily. It faced the darkness of the back room, perched and ready for an altercation.

Agatha heard a low growl from behind the curtain, the same husky voice of Blanche Caillavet. She feared she would never forget it.

"You will never get your Auntie back! Never! And I will come for you when you least expect it. I don't forget. How long can you wait, Agatha Anxious? I have all of eternity." And then a wicked cackle before one long thin arm snatched the cat by the fir of its neck. It let out a hiss and a howl as the arm hurled it toward one of the mirrored walls. It landed on all fours but arched its back, ready for more.

"No!" Agatha screamed, closing her eyes as a deafening cacophony of glass breaking filled her ears. Leopold, half dragging her from the shop, pried her fingers one-by-one from the door, slamming it as hard as he could behind them.

CHAPTER 25
READY

A gatha pedaled hard and fast, holding the coin in a death grip in her fist and not looking to see if Leopold was behind her. She was certain he was, but part of her felt

too afraid to find Blanche Caillavet there too. Beside him and floating with her ragged toes scraping against the concrete, leaving a blood trail behind all three of them.

She knew that wasn't the case. She doubted the old woman could leave the mask shop. *Yet.* Now some of the mirrored walls had broken, and given the right amount of power, stamina, will, and whatever else, Agatha feared Blanche Caillavet's next move.

A tear fell down her cheek, the wind pushing it over to her ear. She hadn't the time to scoop up the white cat on her way out. Leaving it behind pained her in a way she couldn't even think about. She wiped away the tear with the hand that held the coin and pedaled harder. She didn't need Leopold to see her cry.

"You have a duty, Agatha," she whispered to herself, wiping away another tear. "Stay the course."

Her calves were on fire by the time they reached Leopold's house.

She said very little but nodded her head. A silent 'thank you' that Leopold understood. He watched her break into a sprint as she headed toward home. He kept his eyes on her until she was out of his sight.

The house was as dark and silent as she'd left it. Macbeth was sitting right inside the kitchen where she'd left him too, waiting for her to make good on her promise to return. She snuggled him again, this time with a small amount of relief she hadn't had when she'd last seen him.

She again tiptoed across certain floorboards in the living room until she entered her bedroom, immediately throwing off her clothes and putting on a nightgown. In case her parents got up, it would look like she was only having trouble sleeping. Not like she'd been several miles away in the dark on a school night battling an undead former Mardi Gras queen.

Agatha opened her palm again to reveal the coin, which she hadn't let go of since the mask shop. She'd gripped it so hard that some of the design was now imprinted on her skin. She clicked on her bedside lamp and flipped the coin over and over in her hand. It truly was something to marvel at. So old and heavy. Probably worth so much money.

Agatha looked around at her room and sighed. The uneven, dusty baseboards. The windows without locks, the white-painted wood splintering in areas around the frame. Her thoughts drifted to bigger things. No air conditioning in parts of her home, her mother making all her clothes and shoes that needed to be covered in tape and painted, the dryer that never worked, and the clothesline that took days to be effective. Her father working long shifts at the seafood factory, how little she saw him and how much she longed to see him more.

She ran her fingers over the coin again. What problems could this coin solve? She guessed it would help with quite a few.

"Duty," she whispered aloud.

She tucked the coin into her pillowcase and put her head on the pillow. If anyone or anything were to come for it, she'd know.

And Agatha Anxious would be ready for them.

CHAPTER 26
DEFINITELY LOOKING FOR IT

gatha!" Anita Anxious' voice was high and shrill inside Agatha's sleepy head. "You're going to be late! Hurry."

She threw a dress and a pair of stockings on the bed and repeated herself. "Hurry. Hurry."

Agatha rolled over, her squinty eyes barely opening. Her body felt exhausted. She'd only gotten a few hours of sleep. Her hand immediately went to her pillowcase, where she felt the coin's heavy, uneven outline.

"I'm coming. I'm coming," she murmured, throwing her legs over the side of the bed like the two limp, lifeless legs of a mannequin. She groaned, thinking of the spiral-chested white cat from the night before being thrown toward the mirrored walls. A ball of shame formed in her throat that she swallowed away.

"I will get her for you," she whispered, throwing a grey dress over her head and, for the first time, putting the pair of stockings back in her drawer. She looked down at her legs, lily-white and thin. *They need some sun anyway*, she thought.

She went to her desk to gather a few things she'd need for school and stopped. The Scrabble board had changed. Another message for her. The Deer Island Ghost had indeed seen her letters from the night before. This morning, it read:

Agatha's shoulders slumped. Of course, it couldn't be easy. Of course, she couldn't just put the coin on top of the Scrabble board, and that would be the end of it. Of course, she'd have to make a trip to Deer Island to return the coin. Of course! This past week felt an awful lot like being tested, and Agatha was weary. Again, the image of the white cat, its warm, sweet brown eyes staring up at her, flashed through her mind.

"Ok. I'll bring you your coin," she said, grabbing her backpack and slinging it over one shoulder. She retrieved the coin from under her pillow. She couldn't let it out of her sight today. She'd been through too much, and if helping the Deer Island Ghost was one way to weaken the Woman in White, well then, she was going to do it no matter what.

Because she was late, she walked to school by herself, taking her time through the cemetery, pausing at her uncle's grave to give him a small salute. She decided to look over at Blanche Caillavet's grave and noticed the light near her headstone was out. She narrowed her eyes at the grave, feeling the anger swell inside her, and took a deep breath, put one foot in front of the other, and headed toward the school.

She's missed half of her first period, but Mr. Barone—nice as always—gave her a warm smile as she entered his class and found her seat. The room was lively with conversation, and students out of their desks visited each other. Mr. Barone found his way over to her desk.

"I'm giving everyone some free time until the bell rings in a few minutes," he said to her. "Everyone's quiz grades were above a 95 last week, so well deserved." He nodded at her and headed back to his desk, Agatha marveling at what a fantastic teacher he was. So understanding, patient, knowledgeable, and friendly. She doubted any of the high school teachers would be like that.

She headed directly over to Dorian, who was already staring at her, perched on the edge of his seat for a story about the previous night. She nodded toward Leopold, who now joined them, brandishing the silver skeleton key from his pocket.

"Thank you," she said. "Also, we lived through the night." "But what happened?" Dorian said, his ice-blue eyes wide with anticipation. "I mean, you did see *her*, right?" "Yes," Agatha said.

"Ok, so I'm not crazy. Like, she is there, right?" Dorian folded and popped the knuckles of one hand over and over on his knees. *That's his nervous tick*, Agatha thought.

"Yes," Agatha said again. She avoided specifics, especially any heads up about what kind of mess might be at the shop. She cringed at the idea of the mirrors in pieces on the floor and the back room completely in disarray, but she kept her mouth shut, sure that Dorian would mention it at some point.

"Did you get my coin?" he asked her, popping the knuckles of his other hand.

"I did. But it's not your coin," she corrected him.

Dorian stared at her for a few moments, his icy eyes deciding if he had a response.

"It might not be mine, but it's not anybody else's either. Not anybody that's alive anymore and looking for it, anyway."

Leopold cocked his head to one side. "You're partially right on that one," he said, setting the skeleton key on Dorian's desk. "They're not alive, but they're definitely looking for it."

CHAPTER 27
PROPERLY FORMULATING QUESTIONS

"Dorian didn't seem to like my remark too much," Leopold said later in the day as they walked home together.

"No, but we've got to learn to like him a bit better," Agatha responded.

"Why?"

"Because maybe he's a Perceiver, too," she said.

Leopold shrugged. "Just because he saw what he thought was Blanche Caillavet? Like, a glimpse?"

"Yeah? I mean, she is dead, isn't she?" Agatha asked him. "I doubt Dorian Doom is that special."

"Well, I don't know all the requirements for being a Perceiver or what makes us special by any means. Maybe he's not," she said, kicking a small brown rock off the curb and into the road. "But more importantly, you never know when we might need him again."

Leopold shrugged.

"Ok," Agatha said, changing the subject as they neared the edge of the cemetery where she and Leopold usually parted ways, heading to their own respective houses. "We've got to get the coin to Deer Island."

"I figured that," Leopold said, again never surprised at the missions that Agatha threw at him. She liked that. So reliable.

"And it's got to be tonight," she said, hesitant. Maybe that part would irritate him.

"Ok," he responded, unbothered.

Agatha decided to ask. "Why are you always up for whatever I say?"

Leopold was silent, staring down at his white t-shirt, scraping a splotch of dried mustard from it with his finger. "I don't know. Maybe I'm just avoiding my grandfather." He did not meet Agatha's eyes, and she knew he was being honest.

"Ok, we'll have to work on that. Your grandfather is pretty awesome," she said. "But for now, I must focus on returning this coin. Do you have a boat?"

Leopold laughed. "I have bikes, which have been incredibly useful up until now. I guess I'm responsible for providing all our modes of transportation. How about we swim?"

Agatha scoffed. "No way."

Leopold stared at her, waiting for another remark. When none came, he said, "You can't swim, can you, Agatha Anxious?"

Hesitant, she shook her head no. Her parents never had the money to get her proper swim lessons. They had no pool, and the only times she'd really ever swam was during the summer at Hiller Park's community pool, where she generally clung to the ladder or the side of the pool, feeling quite ashamed of herself.

The community pool was gone now, filled in with sand, and turned into a playground. None of her friends or family had pools. And the beach certainly wasn't worth swimming in with its brown, murky water from the Barrier Islands. She'd once heard the water on the other side of the islands was crystal clear. She'd never believed that but also never had the chance to find out either. Maybe tonight, she would.

She tore at a dry piece of skin at her thumb's cuticle. Dry skin was the best. So chewy. Like licorice. If there was no boat and she couldn't swim, how could they get to Deer Island? She was interrupted by Leopold's laughing.

"What?" she said, dropping her thumb to her side and wiping it on her dress.

"Just you," he said, clearly amused. "You nibble when you're thinking. Have you ever noticed that?"

"What's so funny about that," she said, annoyed. They were wasting time.

"Nothing," he said, smirking. "And yes, I have a boat." "Really?"

"Yes," he continued, "It was my grandfather's. My family owns that little pier near the end of my street. The boat is just waiting for us, which suddenly makes me your best friend, I'm guessing."

"Leopold!" she shouted. "We don't have time for this." She playfully punched him in the shoulder as he walked toward Gill Avenue.

"My house. After dark. I'll wait for you, Agatha Anxious," he called after her. "Till the end of time, Agatha Anxious!"

Agatha rolled her eyes but smiled.

CHAPTER 28
IT WAS ME

Agatha busied herself at her desk, finishing up her book report while waiting for her parents to fall asleep. This was becoming quite the routine, waiting on her parents to go to bed so she could sneak out and save the world.

She laughed. She wasn't saving the world, far from it. Maybe just making a small difference in the world of the undead. Keeping the balance. Isn't that what Lucius Nikolai had said? Or was that Aunt Hattie?

She thumbed through the book Leopold had given her the previous week, perusing paragraph after paragraph about the Deer Island Ghost, most of the information very vague. A few sightings. An unnamed pirate. Unspecified treasure. Unknown deckhand. Agatha Anxious could fill in a few of these blanks, but certainly, no one would believe her. She nearly finished the report, purposely leaving the ending undone. After this evening, she could more appropriately fill in the blanks.

She got into bed and turned out her bedside lamp. Still clothed under the covers, she lay on her back, twirling the heavy coin between her fingers. There was a gentle knock at the door, and Agatha could make out her mother's silhouette in the darkness, a loose bun on top of her head that sort of reminded Agatha of Blanche Caillavet. She'd never look at buns the same again.

"Night night, sweetie," her mother whispered into the room.

Agatha wanted to reply but decided against it and instead pretended to be asleep. If her mother knew she was awake, she might stay up longer just to check in on her in another thirty minutes or so. Agatha kept her eyes closed, trying not to let her eyelids flutter, not that her mother could see in the darkness anyway. After a couple more seconds, she heard the door softly shut, her mother telling her father, "I guess she fell asleep."

Bingo.

Again, she waited another thirty to forty-five minutes, making sure her parents were asleep before venturing out.

A brisk run later, she was turning onto Gill Avenue toward Leopold's house when she saw Mr. Dominicus sitting on a folding chair in the corner of the carport. Just then, Leopold appeared from behind the house, carrying a bag of garbage which he dumped into the trash can and pulled to the street, unaware of his grandfather.

Leopold set the garbage can against the curb and noticed Agatha across the street, her round eyes staring from behind the tree trunk. She pointed toward the carport. Leopold looked in the direction of her finger, his body language immediately changing. Agatha saw him crouch behind the trash can, gripping it with trembling hands. He looked back at Agatha, who mouthed, "Get up."

He shook his head.

She tried several more times to get him to stand up, but each time he refused, his shaking knees knocking together in fright. Agatha huffed. She shook her head and strode across the street toward the trash can, her crinkly hair bouncing against her face.

"Mr. Dominicus!" she said from the end of the driveway.

The old man sprang to his feet. "Oh, hi Agatha," he said, unsurprised it was she who was standing in the carport around midnight. *It must run in the family,* she thought. None of them seemed shocked about anything. Ever.

She couldn't very well ask to see Leopold at this hour, although she did wonder if ghosts had any concept of time. Did Mr. Dominicus know it was nearly midnight? Or was this just any other time of day for him? Was his time measured by days and nights and hours, even?

She looked back to the trash can where Leopold still crouched. "Get up," she demanded, looking back toward Mr. Dominicus,

who seemed unconcerned about Agatha.

"I can...can't go over there," he stammered.

"Leopold," she said forcefully. "Why are you so afraid of Mr. Dominicus?"

"Mr. Dominicus?" Leopold said.

"That's what I've always called him. And anyway, that's not the point. What is the problem? He's always been nice to me, and that was before I knew he was a ghost. I don't understand, Leopold," she said, starting to lose her patience with him. "I mean, he can't hurt you. He's not even alive."

Leopold sniffled and crumpled to the ground, his body in a full sitting position now, his head in his hands. "But it was me," he whispered, so softly Agatha could hardly hear him.

"What was you?" she asked, kneeling beside him.

He wiped his nose with the back of his hand, and she saw several tears clinging to his eyelashes. He looked at her. "It was me who killed him."

CHAPTER 29
AN OFFER

It was me," he repeated, in between a few breathy sobs. "And it was an accident."

"How?" Agatha wanted to know.

"A car," he managed, pulling himself together with a few snorts, trying to breathe through his swollen nostrils. "I was about eight, and he was driving. I was trying to show him something in a book of mine and kept begging for him to look. He did and ran off the road."

He buried his face into his knees again, his arms over his head. "We hit a tree."

Agatha let him sob a few more minutes, saying nothing.

"It was my fault," he repeated. "And I'm not sure why he's shown up in the last few years. To haunt me? Maybe that's what I deserve."

"People make mistakes, Leopold," Agatha said, finally. "It sounds like you didn't mean to." Truly, though, she could not fathom the weight of that accident. Leopold didn't want to face his grandfather because of guilt, not because of fear.

"I dunno. Maybe he wants to tell you something?" she offered. It was all she could think of. The Deer Island Ghost sure had a lot to say.

163

Leopold wiped his eyes on the sleeve of his sweatshirt. "We've got to go. It's late already."

"Yeah," she agreed, happy to change the subject. She wasn't good with other people and tears, not even her own. She hated crying. "We've got to get to Deer Island and back before the sun rises."

She turned to get up only to find Mr. Dominicus already behind them both, one hand in his pocket, the other stroking the long braid of his beard.

"Deer Island?" he asked.

"Yes?" she said, looking at Leopold, who couldn't bring himself to look at Mr. Dominicus.

"I can take you," he smiled warmly.

Leopold balked at the idea. If he couldn't face his grandfather in his own bedroom, there seemed to be no way he could sit next to him for a boat ride to Deer Island. Agatha considered arguing about it, but it was now nearly one in the morning. Time was running out, and she was tired.

Leopold ran back to his house to fetch a key, saying nothing to his grandfather.

Agatha knew Deer Island was a short trip from Gill Avenue. Once on the beach, they left their bikes in the sand, navigating their way around the streetlights, attempting to stay in the darkness.

"We'll have to be quick," Leopold said, pointing to the small, ragged pier in front of them where a little aluminum Jon Boat was moored. "I know you can't swim, but can you run?" He snickered as he took off before Agatha could even answer him.

"Funny, funny boy," Agatha said under her breath before breaking into a sprint.

It was quiet this evening, the gulf water barely making a sound as it wrapped itself around the pylons of the pier. No waves. No whitecaps. No wind. Once she reached the boat, Agatha looked off in the distance to her left to see Deer Island, trees lining the horizon, the only thing separating Biloxi from the rest of the Gulf of Mexico. The full moon lay just beyond the tops of the trees, casting a light on the water. Agatha took it as a sign.

"We'll stay in the moonlight," she said to Leopold, who was untying the line which secured the boat to the pier. "It'll lead us straight to the island."

"Let's do it," Leopold said, breathing heavily from the run. "Get in."

"You get in first," she said, scared she'd fall out of it if Leopold weren't already inside the boat.

"You're lighter," he explained. "I can hang onto it while you get in."

She didn't like when he was right. Steadying herself on the end of the pier, she placed her feet into the boat and sort of fell forward, a technique that surprisingly worked. Leopold followed suit after her—rather stealthily, Agatha thought—to avoid losing control of the boat. As he pushed off from the pier, he started the small trolling motor, and Agatha was again thankful for calm waters.

They said nothing for the first few minutes of the trip to Deer Island, Agatha finally breaking the silence. "You need to not be afraid of your grandfather," she said from in front of him, her eyes on the island ahead.

Leopold let out a snort, his eyes on the island too. "And you need to learn to swim."

Silence passed between them before they both broke into raucous laughter—Agatha giggling and Leopold howling—two friends sharing a moment, for the first time unconcerned about their loudness or the lateness of the hour or who would hear them in the middle of the Mississippi Sound on a windless night.

CHAPTER 30
A DUTY, EVEN IN DEATH

The laughing and jokes had ceased by the time their boat nudged the shore of Deer Island; the moonlight had lit a path for them the entire way. Leopold hopped out, soaking his shoes and socks and pulled the boat far onto the shore for fear the tide might come to take it away.

Agatha soaked her shoes too, and she was happy she hadn't worn stockings in the last couple of days. She hated wet clothes and shoes.

Agatha pulled the coin from her backpack. She stood in the sand facing the trees, bushes, and grasses that dotted areas of Deer Island. Agatha wondered what it looked like a hundred years ago when Mary Read landed her pirate ship there. Hurricanes over the centuries had taken their toll on the small island, eroding and changing the land-scape, the brush, and the trees.

Leopold stood beside Agatha, his hands on his hips. "What do we do now?"

"I don't really know," she said. "It's not like we know where the rest of the treasure is."

The light of the moon lit the entire island, another thing Agatha was thankful for, considering neither she nor Leopold remembered a flashlight.

"Let's just wait," she said, taking off her shoes and sitting in the sand, facing back toward Biloxi Beach. Leopold joined her. They watched a few cars pass under the streetlights, which lit up the large antebellum homes behind them. Agatha always said those were the rich people. Any house with columns must mean money. But tonight, under the moon, facing back toward the large homes, she had a different perspective. How happy were these people inside those homes? The homes they had to rebuild every few years when a mighty hurricane came to take all their possessions—including the house—and they couldn't do anything about it?

Agatha thought about her own house. So small but cozy. And really, full of a lot of happiness. She decided she didn't need columns.

"Maybe if you talk to Mr. Dominicus, he'll go away," she said into the wind in front of her.

"What do you mean?" he asked, running his fingers through the sand beside him, scooping up small balls and throwing them into the water ahead of them.

"Ghosts always want something," she turned to him. "Maybe he's hanging around because he wants something from you. And once you talk to him, he'll go away." Although she hated the idea of Mr. Dominicus going away. He was a small connection to Aunt Hattie.

"Yeah, to kill me. That's what he wants. For what I did." He threw another ball of sand into the water, this one with more force than the last.

"No. Mr. Dominicus doesn't seem to be an angry ghost. Was he angry in life?"

Leopold thought for a while, wiping his hands on his shorts. "No. He was great. Happy. Fun. Just......the best."

Agatha saw a tear form in the corner of one of his eyes. She put her hand on his shoulder. "Talk to him. He must want something."

Leopold nodded. "Ok. But only if you learn to swim, Agatha Anxious."

He turned to smile at her when a rustling in the bushes behind them caught their attention. They hopped to their feet, Leopold in a defensive stance though he held no weapon. As they watched, the bushes parted, and they heard steps in the sand, but for a few moments, nothing appeared. Agatha gripped the coin tightly, ready to throw it if necessary at whatever scrambled from the tree line.

What stepped forth, however, was not what either of them expected. Agatha put her hand on Leopold's arm, and he softened his stance. Before them stood a boy, most likely their age. Possibly younger. He was fully clothed—or materialized, as Aunt Hattie would've said—and Agatha was in awe of his attire.

His brown pants were shorter than full length but longer than shorts, ending a little past his knee. A matching flowy brown shirt was tied at the neck with a tattered blazer over top of it, the collar torn and ragged. One side with buttonholes. On the other side, where buttons should've been but had been missing for what Agatha guessed was over a century or two. His long dirty blonde hair hung in curls from a three-pointed black hat that sat atop his head. His cheeks were smudged with a dirty, greasy substance that shined in the moonlight. He was barefoot, his legs covered in the same dirty patches as his face. He smiled but did not talk, simply holding out his hand to Agatha as if he knew why they were there.

Leopold looked at Agatha, who turned the coin over in her palm one last time. She wanted to embed its image in her brain. She might never hold something this valuable in her hand ever again.

Maybe that was a good thing.

She stepped forward and placed the coin in the boy's waiting palm. He wrapped his fingers around it, the same flesh and bone fingers Agatha had seen in her laundry room and at Aunt Hattie's. Now they seemed less monstrous, less threatening, and scary. After all, he was just a boy from another dimension in time, a small blip on the great map of life and death and the afterlife and beyond.

She started to step back toward Leopold, but the boy grabbed her wrist with his other hand. He opened his closed fist where moments before, lay the doubloon. In Agatha's hand, he placed a grey, tarnished piece of glass, smooth and curved on one side, jagged on the other. She curled her fingers around it gently to avoid cutting herself and looked back at the boy, confused. He then handed her a small piece of rolled-up paper, which reminded her of the paper inside the jar she'd first received on her birthday.

Keeping her eyes on the boy, she unrolled the paper. A four-line riddle was written in what she recognized as the boy's childish script:

I'm sometimes where
the old menchat with
big cigars and fancy
hats.

Agatha wrinkled her face. What? It seemed incomplete. "Where is the rest of it?" she asked the boy.

"More to come," he whispered. He placed his finger to his lips and slowly stepped backward. As he did, his clothes disappeared before Agatha's eyes, and so did his skin, revealing a full, small skeleton still holding his bony finger to where his lips had been. As he turned to disappear into the brush, his skull fell from the top of his spine, his right arm catching it in its crook.

"A headless skeleton boy," Agatha whispered to herself.

The boy held his fist in the air as if to thank Agatha and Leopold as his bones crumbled into dust and disappeared before them. The bushes returned to their usual position, and the island was silent except for a few waves lapping the southernmost portion of the island.

Agatha checked her watch as she sat back down on the sand, squishing it between her toes. She faced back toward the beach of Biloxi and, for the first time, realized how beautiful it was. She inhaled, letting the salt-filled air expand her lungs. She thought of the boy she'd just seen, who'd been here long before her and would be long after her.

"Duty," she said aloud.

Leopold was readying the boat, pushing it toward the water's edge. "What?"

She smiled at him and grabbed her shoes. "Nothing."

WITH THE SAME stealth she'd seen earlier, Leopold docked the boat back in its waiting slip. Silently, quickly, perfectly. They rode their bikes back; this time, the ride took much longer, their tired legs and bodies barely able to pedal.

Upon arrival at Leopold's, they parked the bikes in the carport and were bidding each other goodnight when Mr. Dominicus appeared from behind the house. Agatha saw Leopold's body immediately stiffen, but she nudged him.

"Go. Talk. To. Him," she said. She pushed him forward, but he stayed put. Waving at Mr. Dominicus, she walked across the street toward home but decided she was too nosy not to hide behind the tree opposite Leopold's house. She had to watch.

Leopold didn't budge from where he stood, so Mr. Dominicus lumbered over to him. Agatha was too far away to hear them, and after a few minutes, she gave up and started toward home. But not before seeing Leopold mouth the words "I'm sorry," and Mr. Dominicus shake his head. He hugged his grandson, and Leopold returned the gesture, wrapping his grandfather in a tight embrace.

That was good enough for her.

Sometimes those two little *I'm sorry* words are the hardest thing to say.

CHAPTER 31
AN OLD FRIEND

Well, don't you look terrible," Mrs. Wright said to Agatha a few mornings later, trying to squeeze her

hips between the two rows of students as she passed out papers. She was never one for manners.

"Yes, ma'am. I didn't get much sleep this past week," Agatha said, yawning.

"Well, you're first anyway," she said, delighting in her authority and nodding toward the front of the classroom. "For your book report."

Agatha didn't mind. She was used to being first. Her name always pretty much fell first alphabetically in every class. She grabbed her papers from her notebook and jotted a few lines at the bottom in pencil before walking to the front of the classroom. She hated public speaking. Everybody did. But today, she felt more at ease, perhaps because she knew so much about her topic. Or perhaps because a huge weight had been lifted off her shoulders a few nights before. Her duty was done.

She cleared her throat, Leopold staring at her in amusement from the back of the room. She knew he was waiting to see if she'd copied his first few pages.

"My book report was on the Deer Island Ghost," she said. Before she could continue, Mrs. Wright interrupted. "No,

ma'am. Yours was on Blanche Caillavet, I believe?" she said, rummaging through a few pieces of paper on a clipboard.

"Leopold and I switched," Agatha said.

Mrs. Wright was not pleased, her porky mouth turned upside down in a frown, forcing several of her chin rolls together. "Since you and Mr. Panic decided to switch without asking for permission, that'll be minus five points. For *both* of you," she said, narrowing her eyes at Leopold.

"Many years ago," Agatha started, not waiting on Mrs. Wright to continue, "it was rumored that an unknown pirate landed on Deer Island with a treasure. I'm sure many of us have heard about a treasure on Deer Island, right?"

Several heads nodded in the classroom.

"Well, this pirate was actually a woman pirate who dressed as a man, which made many people think she was indeed a man. Her name was Mary Read. She landed on Deer Island with her crew and a treasure in tow. In the golden age of piracy, when pirates controlled the high seas, the treasure consisted of gold coins. I call them doubloons.

"So, Mary decided to bury her treasure on Deer Island, and she asked which of her crew would like to be the one to guard it. A small boy, with golden curls, around the age of fourteen, raised his hand and volunteered. Mary drew her sword and immediately chopped off his head. And they buried his body with the treasure.

"You see, what Mary meant by 'guard the treasure' was really a duty. A pact. To guard the treasure for eternity. And so that's what he does. He guards the treasure, and he's still there guarding it to this day.

"No one has ever found the treasure. Not all of it, at least. But whenever the treasure is disrupted, like if someone finds a coin, the Deer Island Ghost will come to find you, haunting you until you give it back. The end."

She walked briskly back to her desk, not waiting for applause or questions or remarks from Mrs. Wright.

"Well, that was very informative," Mrs. Wright said. "Although it is just a legend, and I'm not sure we really know what pirate landed on

Deer Island and who it was that volunteered or what color hair he had. So, I'm not quite sure where you got your information, but it was entertaining at least." She flashed a smile at Agatha, her mouth so chubby only three of her teeth showed between her lips.

Agatha shot a look at Leopold, whom Mrs. Wright was now selecting as her next victim. She raised her hand. "Mrs. Wright? Can I please go to the bathroom?"

"May I," the teacher corrected her. "And yes, but hurry." Agatha was in no mood to hear any more information about Blanche Caillavet, and she hoped to time her bathroom trip just long enough to miss Leopold's report.

When Agatha reached the door, she turned back toward her teacher, who was scratching the area around her belly button. "I got my information from Miz Honeysuckle," she said to Mrs. Wright and the rest of the classroom, her voice starting to break. "The most reliable source there ever was," she said before exiting the hallway.

CHAPTER 32
LIT AND LINGERING

A storm was brewing as Agatha Anxious cut through Biloxi Cemetery on her way home, this time alone as Leopold had been picked up from school by his mother for a

dentist appointment. She passed a few headstones, reading the names and making up a few stories in her head about their demise.

The Ainsworth grave. She remembered having joked about it to Leopold on the first day they started talking. She bent down and picked up a few rotten silk flowers from in front of the tomb. Apparently, it hadn't been visited in quite a while. *Nothing sadder than a forgotten grave*, she thought.

She was in the middle of thinking about how well taken care of her uncle's grave was when she noticed movement over by his headstone. She froze where she stood and waited. Two white paws appeared, and then a head.

The cat from the mask shop.

Agatha squealed to herself but didn't want to frighten the cat. Slowly, she walked over to the back of her uncle's grave, gently setting down her backpack in front of his headstone and kneeling by the cat. She offered her hand.

"Aunt Hattie?" she whispered.

The cat looked at her, its warm brown eyes embracing hers for a few moments before it rammed its head into her palm. She scooped it up in a long hug, a few tears falling from her cheeks onto its fur. It laid its head on Agatha's shoulder, and she understood at that moment that Aunt Hattie wasn't coming back. This creature, in her arms, was Aunt Hattie for the foreseeable future.

A sudden crack of thunder interrupted their reunion, and the cat sprang from her arms, running toward Agatha's backyard on Azalea Street, where it stopped to look back at her. Agatha knew stood the cat would be waiting for her when she got home. She nodded and wiped the corners of her eyes. She would rather have her aunt in this form than not have her aunt at all.

She watched the cat turn and weave through a few headstones until it disappeared from her view. How had Aunt Hattie escaped? Perhaps she'd weakened Blanche Caillavet by returning the coin to the Deer Island Ghost. Lucius Nikolai had been very strange, but he'd been of some assistance, alluding to Blanche's weakness with her reflection and urging her to stay the course.

She turned back toward her uncle's grave, wiping away some loose grass cuttings and making sure the small, plastic American flag was firmly planted in the ground next to the headstone. She wanted to glance in the direction of Blanche Caillavet's grave over in the cemetery corner but decided against it.

Just then, a strong breeze whispered through the trees, rustling the leaves and moss-like tendrils of hair on the surface of a skull. She criss-crossed her body with her arms, studying the sky, wondering how long before the rain would appear. She hoped it would be a good storm.

She'd better get home.

She reached for her backpack in front of Uncle Tim's grave, but something moved in her periphery. A small gasp caught in her throat, but Agatha swallowed it away as she slowly stepped away from his headstone, facing the mausoleum she'd tried so hard to ignore.

The wind whipped past her left and right, urging her to hurry. Agatha's short blonde hair blew in her face and stuck to her lips, but she made no move to push it away. She heard the leaves rattle over the ground, scurrying in all different directions like the roaches in her laundry room. Her arms filled with goosebumps, and the skeleton hand of chills crept up her spine, counting her ribs and winding its way to the back of her neck, where it seemed to grip her in a warning.

She heard Blanche Caillavet's growl and cackle and her final, wicked words. They were less of a threat and more of an ominous promise.

How long can you wait, Agatha Anxious? I have all of eternity.

Fully facing the stone sepulcher, Agatha saw its iron gate was now ajar, moving back and forth slightly with the heavy wind, an ache coming from its joints. Someone else might have easily mistaken the door being open for the age of the crypt or perhaps the work of graverobbers. But not Agatha Anxious.

She knew the door symbolized much more than just a rusty closure with weakened hinges. She knew the door separated good from bad. Death from afterlife. A thin, passable veil that served as the balance between two vastly different worlds, a portal that allowed danger to cross over to the world of the living.

As she watched, a frail hand with grey fingernails reached from within the crypt and slowly closed the iron door before disappearing into the darkness.

And the cemetery light, perfectly placed in front of the marble structure bearing the name Blanche Caillavet, flickered on.

EPILOGUE

The rest of October, November, and December flew by quite quickly. Agatha decided to dress as a white cat for Halloween, happily painting a black spiral onto her

white leotard. She had the fleeting thought of being too old for Halloween costumes but quickly dismissed it. Never.

"Ooh, nice design," her mother had said, clueless.

Leopold dressed in a checkered shirt with suspenders and jeans, painting a fake beard onto his face. His teachers and classmates said he was a lumberjack. He said he was something else— a tribute of a sort.

By Christmas, another of her father's sisters, Aunt Letty, had taken over Hattie's Odds & Ends. She was also living in Aunt Hattie's house, taking care of the white cats—at Agatha's insistence. Agatha didn't know her well. She'd left the coast years ago rather quickly and mysteriously, and she didn't come to holiday gatherings. She wasn't the unique, quirky, colorful figure Hattie Anxious was, but she was peculiar and mystifying in her own right. A buxom woman with blonde hair and green eyes, Aunt Letty only wore black lace outfits, something Agatha appreciated. *Every family has its secrets*, Agatha thought. And not just families. Every *person* has their secrets, too.

Though life continued for the Anxious family, certainly no one forgot Aunt Hattie, and tears were sometimes shed behind closed doors or at night or in the shower. Agatha, however, couldn't be too sad about it as she curled up with a white spiral-chested cat every evening whom she'd named Marigold only because Hattie would've been too obvious and weird.

She vowed to herself to somehow, someday, make The Woman in White pay for what she'd done to her aunt, though she wasn't sure how it could be done. She'd have to make another visit to Lucius Nikolai for that.

On Christmas morning, Agatha waited until she heard her parents at the coffee maker before making an appearance in the living room, Marigold cradled in her arms. As usual, Agatha doled out the Christmas presents to each member of the family, stacking her five presents in a neat pile and waiting her turn before ripping the wrapping paper to shreds. Three dresses, one pair of shoes, two bracelets made of shells, several erasers that smelled like grape, strawberry, and lemon, and a crossbody purse. Later, Agatha sipped on a mug of warm hot chocolate as her mother prepared their Christmas breakfast. Satisfied with her presents-though, the dresses still had no pockets-Agatha sat back against the Anxious family's maroon velvet couch, sniffing away at the erasers, when her father appeared in the living room.

He laid a single square box on her lap. "This is yours," he said, a smile laced with a distinct amount of sadness.

"The best for last?" she asked, lifting the box, excited by its heaviness.

He nodded. "The very best for last."

She decided to be gentle, softly tearing the wrapping paper where it was taped. She reached inside the cardboard box and pulled out an item she'd seen before. Many times but never touched nor opened it.

Aunt Hattie's golden box.

Her eyes widened with surprise; she looked at her father, who shrugged. "I don't understand the note inside, but I guess she wanted you to have it. Letty gave it to me a few weeks ago. There's no reason it should be at the shop. It's been sitting on her desk for years."

For years, Agatha knew that to be true, remembering all the times she'd begged Aunt Hattie to touch it or open it or tell her what sort of surprises lay inside.

Agatha thought for a moment. "Can I open this in my room?" she asked.

"Of course," her father said, patting her on the knee.

Agatha sprang from the couch toward her room, shutting the door behind her. She sat on her bed, the box balanced on her lap. She lifted the small latch on the front of the box before gripping the heavy lid with both hands and opening it. Black velvet covered the inside of the box, a single handwritten note on top of an item wrapped in newspaper.

Agatha picked up the note, written in the lovely, shaky script of her aunt. She knew what it said before reading it.

My dearest Agatha,

Someday you'll need this and someday it'll be yours, is what I've always said. That day is today, and the time is soon.

I love you always and Ruff's is better, Aunt Hattie

Agatha ran her fingers over the script, feeling the indentation in the paper. She picked up the item wrapped inside the newspaper. She turned it over in her hands, trying to guess what lay beneath the wrapping. Oddly shaped, oval in some areas, pointed in others. And long and thin in another area.

Finally, she tore off the paper to reveal an ornate silver hand mirror, obviously from long ago. The back of the mirror was a cat face, the silver tarnished in between the eyes, the whiskers, the sides of its nose, and the inner parts of its ears, giving it a menacing appearance and a nefarious grin. The plain silver handle was also tarnished but flat, smooth, and not nearly as ornate as the back. Agatha could see why. She rubbed her thumb across the handle to reveal an engraving from long ago, the dark color of corrosion caught in between two uppercase cursive letters:

B.C.

Agatha turned the mirror over to discover the mirror glass was missing. A breath caught in her throat, and she yanked open her nightstand drawer, grabbing her jewelry box. Inside, she slowly picked up the piece of jagged mirror glass she'd been given by the Deer Island Ghost. She studied the mirror for a few moments before deciding to lay it softly on the far left, inside the mirror's empty frame.

A perfect fit.

Where were the other pieces? How many were left before the mirror was complete again? And how in the world would she find them? Suddenly, a single number popped into her head—a memory.

Chalk and ash. A fire. Blackened eyes and Converse shoes. A chat, a taste, a truth. And the whitish lips and reptilian tongue from which the word was spoken.

Five.

"Five Deadfellows," she said aloud. "Five pieces."

She ran through the living room and kitchen, past her mother, who was cooking eggs and bacon, and Macbeth, who slept under her feet. She bounded down the back steps and over toward Gill Avenue, where she pounded her fists against Leopold's front door, not caring whether he was in the middle of opening presents or still sleeping or eating his Christmas breakfast.

He answered the door in his pajamas, a collared, button-up sleep shirt, and long pants both with blue and white stripes, a sight Agatha hadn't seen before. As usual, he was not surprised to find her at his door. He rubbed his eyes.

"Well, Merry Christmas, Agatha. And what is that?" he said, pointing to the shiny object she held in her hands.

She nodded her head, a sarcastic smile spreading over her little pink lips. Placing the cat mirror in his hands with a little too much force, she pointed at the initials.

"Four ghosts to go."

ACKNOWLEDGMENTS

My family has greatly contributed to the freedom and space to live a life creating spooky things, eagerly devouring each new ghastly tale or macabre idea. For this, I thank you.

Thank you to my early reviewers who found things my author's eyes could not see and ultimately helped in crafting a solid piece of middle-grade horror.

To my fellow Biloxians: This book is based largely on my childhood (people, experiences, descriptions of my childhood home and middle school, and yes, the Thanksgiving Roach). There are little pieces of nostalgia in this book, places that no longer exist thanks to Hurricane Katrina. These gems are written specifically for you. May you always know we have the best hometown on the planet, one which no hurricane will ever take away.

And lastly, my readers: Those who welcome the chills down your spine, the inability to sleep after a creepy book, the moody, the morbid, and macabre. Those who HOPE to find something lurking under their beds in the darkness: I am at your service...

Stay strange.

NOW...
Turn the page for a special preview of

AGATHA ANXIOUS
& THE
BACK BAY HAUNTING

CHAPTER 1
THE SUMMONING

Tippy Trinkle slid her tiny body out from between her silken sheets until her toes touched her carpet. She knelt beside her four-poster bed, pulling a small wooden box out from the darkness. Her fingers touched the initials on the box's top, and she chewed her lip, deciding whether to proceed. Reaching under the bed again, she pulled out a small stash of items she'd hidden after breakfast that morning, items sure to garner her a punishment if her mother knew of their existence: a small black candle, a set of matches, and a leatherbound little book titled *J. Wiltz's Guide for Summoning the Dead.*

She'd found the book at the weird gift shop on the beach. Hattie's Odds & Ends or something, although it was no longer run by Ms. Hattie, Tippy knew. Instead, it was managed by Agatha Anxious' other aunt, the more serious one, whatever her name was.

Tippy didn't have money for the book, but she'd found an item under $2 and being a master of distraction, had chatted up the aunt at the checkout—Aunt Less Friendly—as she'd slyly slipped the book in the waistband of her jeans. Now fingering its worn cover, Tippy felt a pang of regret for stealing it. Short-lived it was though, as she decided her purpose outweighed the crime.

She chose to sit in her closet, since it offered no light. Tippy lived in one of the old, antebellum homes on Biloxi Beach, and the moonlight reflected off the water, making her bedroom far too bright for a task such as hers. Two strikes against the side of the matchbox and her candle flickered to life, its wooden wick crackling and sparking in the darkness. "Dark Library," the candle was called, and it smelled as musty as its title suggested. Another small trinket she took from Hattie's Odds & Ends.

Tippy studied the cover of the book. She wondered where it had been during its lifetime, and how many souls it had summoned back to the earth. Awakened from their coffin slumbers for purposes only known to the summoner.

What is my purpose? Tippy asked herself. For the last month, the ache of wanting to see her twin again nearly consumed her. Hardly any of Tippy's friends knew she'd had a twin. It wasn't something she discussed. But every now and then, and more often than she expected, the want of communication was so strong, she could hardly stand it.

It started three weeks ago when she'd found the toy. A pair of hugging pandas whose hands were magnetic and could be separated or attached. Most often, the pandas had been separated. Her twin had one, and Tippy had the other. Tippy had begged to have one panda placed in the coffin at the funeral home, but her mother had refused and kept them both in her room, long forgotten by Tippy until recently when she found them in her mother's closet. Since then, the need to see her twin had been nearly unbearable.

Tippy opened the book to the table of contents and scanned until she saw "The Act of Summoning" chapter, deciding she didn't need to read all the fluff chapters before it. *Let's get to it*, she thought.

She skimmed the chapter, hitting the important steps and closed the book with a thud. Opening the wooden box, she pulled out a few of her twin's belongings she'd saved. A poem on notebook paper, a favorite book, a t-shirt, the panda, and lastly, his birth and death certificates, both of which she'd stolen from her father's office. She was getting good at stealing things.

"Henry Trinkle," she said. The candle crackled behind her whisper. She held her hand over the open flame until it hurt, immediately placing her open palm on the book.

"November 7th," she said. *(Birthday)*

"June 11th." *(Death date)*

"February 21st." *(Today's date)*

"I want to see you." *(Reason for summoning)*

Silence.

She repeated it twice more, each time holding her palm over the open flame until it hurt. "November 7th. June 11th. February 21st. I want to see you. November 7th. June 11th. February 21st. I want to see you." And with a breath, she extinguished the candle.

Darkness enveloped her like a cloak, and she sat perfectly still, the white noise of nothingness loud in her ears. Tippy listened for any sign but was met with silence. She sat cross legged in the dark turning the matchbox over and over in between her fingers.

"Henry?" she whispered.

The air seemed to change in the small space of the closet. A rusty hanger above her shifted ever so slightly, scraping metal on metal, and she felt one of her hanging dresses brush her shoulder.

"Henry?" she said again, louder, fumbling to light a single match. The flame overtook the darkness, and Tippy saw she was alone. "Forget it," she huffed, throwing everything back in the wooden box. She kicked open the closet door with her foot and tossed the matches in the garbage can under her desk. With a sigh, she slid back into bed, throwing the covers over her head.

Tippy Trinkle lay on her back, deep in thought, her eyes clenched shut until she fell asleep, unaware of the evil which crept from the closet like a mist, floating through her bedroom, fingering the heavy fabric of her curtains, rustling the pages of the journal on her nightstand until it came to settle under the bed with an angry, little growl.

AGATHA ANXIOUS

& THE
BACK BAY HAUNTING

by

RJ McDOWELL

Book 2 of **The Deadfellow Five**

COMING MARCH 2026!

WYATT & SONS
PUBLISHERS, LLC

ABOUT THE AUTHOR

RJ MCDOWELL grew up in Biloxi, Mississippi, with a vivid imagination and an imaginary friend, both of which followed her into adulthood. She adores all things spooky and pens her creepy stories by candlelight. She lives in a house she calls McDowell Manor, where she eats black licorice and is still afraid of the closet monster. She hopes her readers like the dark as much as she does.

facebook.com/RJMcDowell

instagram.com/rjmcdowellauthor

tiktok.com/@rjmcdowellauthor

You have a story.
We want to publish it.

Everyone has as a story to tell. It might be about something you know how to do, or what has happened in your life, or it may be a thrilling, or romantic, or intriguing, or heartwarming, or suspenseful story, starring a cast of characters that have been swimming around in your imagination.

And at Wyatt & Sons Publishers, we can get your story onto the pages of a book just like the one you are holding in your hand. With professional interior design and a custom, professionally designed cover built just for you from the start, you can finally see your dream of being an author become reality. Then, you will see your book listed with retailers all over the world as people are able to buy your book from wherever they are and have it delivered to their home or their e-reader.

So what are you waiting for? This is your time.

visit us at

www.wyattpublishing.com

for details on how to get started becoming a
published author right away.